RUSH TO JUDGEMENT

A DCI HARRY MCNEIL NOVEL

JOHN CARSON

DCI HARRY MCNEIL SERIES
Return to Evil
Sticks and Stones
Back to Life
Dead Before You Die
Hour of Need
Blood and Tears
Devil to Pay
Point of no Return
Rush to Judgement
Against the Clock

Where Stars Will Shine – a charity anthology
compiled by Emma Mitchell, featuring a
Harry McNeil short story –
The Art of War and Peace

DCI SEAN BRACKEN SERIES

Starvation Lake

Think Twice

DI FRANK MILLER SERIES

Crash Point

Silent Marker

Rain Town

Watch Me Bleed

Broken Wheels

Sudden Death

Under the Knife

Trial and Error

Warning Sign

Cut Throat

Blood from a Stone

Time of Death

Frank Miller Crime Series – Books 1-3 – Box set
Frank Miller Crime Series - Books 4-6 - Box set

MAX DOYLE SERIES
Final Steps
Code Red
The October Project

SCOTT MARSHALL SERIES

Old Habits

RUSH TO JUDGEMENT

Created with Vellum

This one is for Bejay Roles

ONE

He held the knife aloft, watching the man's back. He gently ran the tip of the blade along the kitchen island's marble top, not making a sound, slowly advancing on the man in front of him.

He held it high, the steel glinting in the subdued lighting. He took another step, getting closer.

Then, without warning, the man turned towards him and looked at the deadly weapon.

'Jesus, Shug, you'll do yourself a mischief there,' Muckle McInsh said.

'I'm starving. Has he not moved yet?'

Muckle looked back at the fridge, then down at the floor where his dog lay. Sparky lifted his head as if he knew the two men were talking about him, then laid it back down again.

'He moves his heid to look at us, then goes back to

doing his own thing. He's like this at home as well. Need to get into the dishwasher? Dug's lying in front of it. Need the lav? Dug's lying on the tile floor, cooling off. The only time he moves is when the wife gets the hoover out because he's feared o' it. I swear the bugger's doing it on purpose.'

'They left us that turkey for a midnight snack, and correct me if I'm wrong, but it's twelve fifteen in the a.m.'

'Come on, Sparks, get your arse in gear, boy,' Muckle said. No joy. The German shepherd lay where he was, blocking the doors to the large built-in fridge. Beyond the stainless steel waited a turkey with their name on it.

'I meant to ask what you got me for Christmas,' Shug said, putting the knife down before he managed to cut off a valuable piece of himself.

'I got you something from the FcCall line,' Muckle replied.

'FcCall? Never heard of it.'

'More popularly known as fuck all.'

'Ah. Covering up your stinginess with humour. Very classy.'

'What's classy?' a female voice said from behind them. Vern Baxter, the only female member of the security team.

'Muckle's subtle way of telling me that he's a skinflint.'

She smiled at the smaller man. 'Some people call it being wise.'

And with the sound of her voice, Sparky got up and went over to her, his tail wagging.

'Now you get up, ya hoor,' Muckle said quietly, pulling one half of the fridge open. 'You up for a sandwich, Miss Vern?' he said, taking the turkey-laden tray out and putting it on the counter. It never failed to amaze him how big the kitchen was. His whole flat could fit in it.

'Don't mind if I do,' she said, pausing from petting the dog and making baby noises at him. 'And I'm sure my little friend here wouldn't mind a few bits.'

'I must admit I am famished,' Shug said.

'She meant Sparky,' Muckle said without turning round.

Shug looked at Vern. 'Say it's not true.'

'Sorry, but my furry friend looks at me longingly and my heart melts.' More rubbing his sides and talking to him like he was a baby.

'Hey, Muckle, if I wear a fur coat, will you put some turkey on a plate for me?' Shug asked.

'Yeah, fuc...I mean, watch me.' Muckle brought the bird out and felt his stomach rumbling. 'Our Christmas dinner. What a beauty.'

'If he has any more turkey, he'll crash out,' Shug said. 'And don't get me started on the dog.'

'You're hilarious, Shug. I can eat a horse and still go a full shift.'

The other two looked at him.

'Not that I've ever eaten a horse, mind. But this frame is built for eating and I can still go the full nine yards.'

'Getting your metaphors mixed up there, Muckle,' Vern said.

'You know what I'm talking about there, Miss Vern. Not an ounce of fat on me. It's taking Fuzzy Bum there on a three-mile walk every day. He goes up to our room, lies down in front of the fire and that's him till work time. Me? I'm a machine.'

'Well, get cutting that bird up. I only had a little bit of dinner,' Vern said, watching as Sparky went into begging mode and sat looking at his master.

'I only had a turkey sandwich earlier. I've been imagining this moment for hours now,' Muckle said.

He was about to stick the carving knife in when they all heard a scream coming from outside.

Sparky turned away from Muckle and started barking ferociously, sensing something was up.

Muckle put the knife down. 'Come on, Shug, let's go and see what's up.' He grabbed Sparky's lead off the counter and clipped it on him. The big dog started yanking him towards the kitchen door.

'That's it, boy, let's go,' he said. Then, in a lower voice: 'Ease up for fuck's sake, or you'll have me on my arse.'

'You stay here, Miss Vern,' Shug said, making sure his extendable baton was in his inside pocket. He grabbed his torch from the counter and went to follow Muckle outside.

'So I will,' she replied. 'I'm coming with you. No arguments.' She grabbed the carving knife and Shug tried not to let his eyes go wide.

They left the kitchen and went along the back corridor, where Muckle was now standing with the door wide open. They all heard another scream, then it was choked off.

'It's coming from the woods,' Shug said, catching up with Muckle and Vern.

Another scream, not as loud this time.

'Let's go up the path into the Magic Woods,' Vern said.

Both security men turned to look at her. *Magic Woods?*

Vern shrugged. 'It's what I heard one of the staff call them. Across the back lawn and there's an opening in the trees.'

Sparky was already pulling in that direction as

both men switched their torches on. The place was covered in a foot of snow, making it lighter than normal, and the beams of light danced around as they started moving as fast as they could.

'Do either of you have a spare torch?' Vern asked. 'I forgot to grab mine.'

Shug turned to look at her and his light bounced off the sharp steel in her hand. *You didn't forget to grab a fucking knife, though.* 'Here, I have a small one in my pocket as well as this big one.'

He fished it out and handed it over before moving forward, grateful that Vern was now in front of him, her weapon of mass destruction pointed at Muckle's back and not his.

They reached the pathway and continued on into the woods. There were no footprints here and it was starting to get treacherous, though the dog seemed to thrive in these conditions.

Sparky pulled harder and Muckle felt himself losing his footing, the dog's lead in one hand and his torch in the other, the light now illuminating the branches and the leaves, anywhere but the ground in front of him.

'Sparky, if you pull me over and make me a laughing stock, I swear I'll send your new fucking ball back to the shop, Christmas present or no Christmas present.'

Muckle slipped and fell on his face. Sparky could haul his master, but he couldn't drag him, so he stopped, panting. 'Aw, fucking magic, eh?'

'There's no time for a lie-down, lazy bugger,' Shug said, stopping behind Vern, glad to see she hadn't also slipped and pinned Muckle to the ground by the goolies with her knife.

'Bastard ground's slippy,' Muckle said, getting to his knees, then standing up. 'Pardon the French, Miss Vern,' he said, throwing a look at Shug that suggested the grin on his face might be getting wiped off shortly.

And Sparky was off again, barking and growling. Muckle let out some more of the long lead and then they were in a clearing. It was darker in here, the snow not reaching the ground as much as outside.

What seemed like a shadow at first started to move. A figure stood looking at the woman hanging from an overhanging branch. He turned to look at the advancing figures before turning away and cresting the brow of the pathway.

'Hey, fucking stop right there!' Muckle shouted, which revved the dog up more. 'I'll let the dog go!'

But he had no intention of letting Sparky run off after the stranger. Instead, they turned their attention to the female who was hanging limply from the tree.

'Out my way,' Vern said, following the line of the

rope to where it was tied to another tree, holding the woman up.

Vern sliced into the rope with her knife, back and forward like a saw, and strands starting snapping. She worked hard at it until the rope broke and the woman fell to the ground.

Shug was on the phone, calling it in. Muckle looked around them, but was confident that nobody would be able to sneak up on them with the dog in a frenzy.

Vern kneeled beside the woman, trying to get the rope off, while Muckle grabbed hold of Sparky's K9 vest on the back and settled him. He bent over and looked at the woman and put a hand on Vern's shoulder.

'She's gone,' he said.

'Oh my God,' Vern said in a voice barely above a whisper.

Shug walked over. 'Uniforms will be on their way over, but a pound to a penny there are no detectives round here.'

'They'll draft them in from Inverness, no doubt,' Vern said.

'I've got a better idea,' Muckle said, taking his phone out.

He called the one person in the world whom he trusted more than anything.

TWO

DCI Jimmy Dunbar was sitting drinking coffee with a female DS when the man with the ponytail and beard walked in. Dunbar had been sitting on the edge of a desk and was immediately on his feet, as were some of the other officers.

'You can't come in here, pal,' Dunbar said, getting ready to share the contents of his mug with Beardie's face.

'It's me, sir. DS Evans. You told me to report here this morning.'

Dunbar had to look twice as the other detectives relaxed. Evans had long, straggly hair pulled back into a ponytail and a beard that no self-respecting tramp would be seen dead with.

'What the bloody hell happened to you?' Dunbar asked.

'You know I broke my ankle and I've been off for six weeks –'

'Alright, Tweedledum, I know that. I meant what's with the Billy Connolly look?'

'It's the new me. What can I say?'

'You can say you bumped your heid when you fell down the flight of stairs. You can say you're going home to shave and get a haircut.'

'No can do. My new girlfriend said it makes me look manly.'

'Fucking mangy, more like.'

Evans smiled. 'I did some thinking while I was off. Maybe the polis isn't for me.'

Dunbar put his mug down and guided Evans out into the corridor and along to the canteen. 'You need a coffee.'

'I don't. I watch what I eat and drink now. No sugar.'

'Jesus.'

'Why are we in here on Boxing Day anyway? I had plans.'

'What kind of plans?' Dunbar punched the buttons on the machine after putting money in.

'Just plans with Linda.'

'She thinks this is okay? Look at the state of you. Did you have a pagger with Santa or something? Your bloody hair's all over the place and you look like shite.'

'The Christmas spirit certainly doesn't hang around in your house, does it?'

Dunbar took the coffee cup and handed it to Evans. 'This is not my house. And I managed to get up and dressed this morning without looking like a mangy dug.'

'I washed my hair.'

Dunbar sighed. 'Listen, son, you don't have much luck with women, I know that. But the right lassie will come along. You don't want to be hanging out with some hippie who wants to change your whole life. Have I ever steered you wrong?'

'Naw, but Linda's keeping me right. She spent the night.'

'What did your mother have to say about that?'

'She's away staying at my auntie's house. I told her I'd be fine on Christmas and she wasn't going to go without me at first, but I persuaded her.'

'And Linda the cleaning lady came round to dust some of your silverware.'

'She polished more than that.'

'That's enough, manky bastard. I don't want any sordid details.'

'She's terrific, even though she's a bit older than me.'

'Grab a granny? Somehow that doesn't surprise me. You've been plumbing the depths for a while now.'

'Age doesn't matter. We have a connection,' Evans said.

'You have a bank account.'

'It's not like that.'

They left the canteen, Evans blowing on the coffee in the plastic cup in the hope it would taste less like dirty rainwater, and they headed upstairs.

'What's it like, son?' Dunbar said. 'She gives you a good time, you blow your life savings on her and then she's off to the next mug?'

'Nothing like that.'

'You help her spend her pension money every week?'

'She used to be known as Luscious Linda,' Evans said.

'And now it's just Lush?'

'What we have is real. She has a completely different outlook on life.'

'You said that about that other lassie and it turned out she was married.' Dunbar shook his head.

'You've got to have rain to see the rainbow,' Evans replied.

'What the fuck does that mean?'

'I don't know. I heard it on TV.'

'I hope you didn't go buying her a diamond ring for Christmas?'

Evans sipped some of the coffee and looked away.

'Please tell me you're not that daft,' Dunbar said.

Still no answer.

'Can I have that five hundred quid back that I lent you last summer?'

'What five hundred quid?' Evans said.

'I'm just trying to see how gullible you are.'

'It was a friendship ring, alright? Nothing more.'

'Does it come with a copy of your American Express card?'

'Listen, boss, after all the bad luck I've had with women, I'm just playing it easy with Linda. I'm learning things about myself.'

'How old is she?'

Evans mumbled something.

'What?' Dunbar said.

'Forty. Fifty. Age is just a number.'

'Fifty? Tell me you're fucking joking.'

'I also said forty. It could be either.'

'What's her last name?'

'Fry,' Evans said.

'Linda Fry?'

'Aye. You know her?'

'Give me one good reason I shouldn't kick you in the bollocks right now. As things are going, I don't think I would want you bringing another eejit into the world.'

'I'm just having fun, Jimmy. Besides, you've had your fair share of doing daft things.'

'Name fucking one.'

'I can't offhand, but there have been plenty of times —'

Dunbar held up a hand. 'Stop talking.'

'Just saying.'

'Don't just say. I've heard enough of you saying.'

Evans drank some more of the tasteless liquid. 'Anyway, boss, I'm glad you're still in the holiday mood, wearing your ugly sweater.'

'This is my normal sweater, cheeky bastard.'

'Oh, right. I thought Oxfam had a sale on or something.'

'Listen, until you get your fucking hair sorted, don't try to divert my attention from you having it away with "Let's Be Having You" Linda.'

A uniformed sergeant was walking towards them. 'I haven't heard that name in a long time,' he said, smiling.

Dunbar just nodded to him as he passed.

Evans looked puzzled. 'He knows her?'

'Everybody in the station knows Linda. I haven't personally been properly introduced, as it were, but you go for it, son. Her catchphrase used to be, *Come Fry with me*.'

'She told me about that. Because she was a flight attendant.'

Dunbar laughed. 'No, son, she used to say that because she worked in the chippie along the road and it was appropriate since her last name is Fry. She was never a bloody flight attendant.'

'She's the station bike?'

'I'm not saying anything more about your girl-friend. Except one thing: she was around here when you were still in high school.'

'Aw fuck. She never said.'

'She collects coppers like some women collect recipes. And let me tell you something: she's older than me. She left fifty behind a long time ago.'

Evans looked at the floor, where he expected a big hole to appear so he could jump into it. 'What am I going to do now?'

'Look for the rainbow.'

They stopped outside the incident room.

'Don't tell anybody, Jimmy, for God's sake.'

'My lips are sealed. But come on, Stewart's in my office,' Dunbar said. Detective Superintendent Calvin Stewart, their boss.

'Why's he in there?'

'You'll see. Muckle McInsh called me last night and I called Stewart. He said to bring you in today.'

'It's Boxing Day. I had plans.'

'If they're with Linda, I think you should tell her duty calls. We'll be going away.'

'I will. I'll tell her I've been transferred to Kathmandu or something.'

'Do whatever it takes, son. She'll use you, then she'll be on to the next mug.'

'I had fun with her, I have to admit.'

'Look to settle down with somebody. That lassie in CID I was talking to, she split up with her boyfriend a couple of months ago and she was asking what your situation was.'

'Really?' Evans said. 'Did you tell her I was single?'

'What is it they say on Facebook? *It's complicated.* But now you've walked in looking like that, I'd be surprised if Bigfoot wanted to go out with you.'

They went into the incident room, filled with the same on-call CID officers, and saw Stewart across in Dunbar's office. Dunbar walked over to his office and knocked on the door, which was slightly ajar.

Stewart was sitting in Dunbar's chair, wearing an ugly Christmas sweater with flying snowmen.

'Fucking jumper. It's almost as bad as yours, Jimmy. Who started this craze anyway?'

'I wish I knew. They're making a fortune.' Dunbar and Evans sat down on the other two chairs. Dunbar noticed Stewart had plasters on three of his fingers.

'You know what my wife got me for Christmas?' Stewart said.

They both shook their heads.

'Divorce papers.' Stewart held up a hand. 'I know what you're going to say.'

Why did it take her so long?

'How could she leave a machine like this?' Stewart finished before either detective could answer. 'That's what I thought. But she is. And you know what her parting shot was? You couldn't burn your blinds with a fucking lighter.'

Dunbar looked at his blinds. Some of the slats were melted. He looked over at Evans as if he couldn't believe his eyes and needed the younger detective to confirm what he was seeing.

'Well, I fucking showed her, eh?'

'Aye, you certainly did that,' Dunbar said. 'But I'm assuming you wanted to see us after my phone call last night?'

'Oh aye, that. Michael McInsh's phone call.' Everybody Dunbar knew called DI Michael McInsh 'Muckle', because of the big man's size, but obviously Stewart didn't.

The superintendent carried on. 'You told me some fucker hanged a lassie in the trees on some estate he's working at. I got on the phone to the local sergeant. Right stroppy bastard he was. Lucky you're the one going up or else I'd...' Stewart looked at the wall for a moment, thinking of some imaginary punishment he'd inflict on the unsuspecting uniform.

'Burn his blinds?' Dunbar said.

'What? Oh, fuck, there you go. Maybe burn the whole station down. Get a good fire going. Anyway, he whined about us going up north. He told me in no uncertain terms that they have real police officers up there who are perfectly capable of doing the job. Why is it those little pissant stations are run by a uniform who thinks he's Columbo?'

'And you told him?'

'I told him I'd kick his bollocks if he ever used that tone with me again. Then I said both of you and two of Lothian and Borders' finest were going up to start the investigation.'

Dunbar wondered if Stewart would ever get used to the fact that Scotland had a unified police force now. The Lothian and Borders name had been sucked up into the pile along with every other police force in Scotland, and now they were one big, happy family. Except for a uniformed sergeant somewhere up north.

'Where's the place again?' Stewart said.

'Blairgowan,' Dunbar said. 'Near the Cairngorms. Not to be confused with Blairgowrie.'

'Aye, that's it. Get up there with that scruffy bastard and see what's going on. Harry McNeil and that wife of his are going too. I spoke to my counterpart in Edinburgh – I think he was more pished than I was last night – and he agreed we should get up there. Then I called my boss and he did whatever it is he does, which I think involves a pack of tarot cards, and here we are. Inverness have a serial rapist and he's just killed a lassie, so they don't have the manpower to go down there. I hope you had a nice Christmas break; looking at that paraffin lamp there, I'm guessing he didn't get an electric razor for a present.'

'Well, since it's Boxing Day, I sort of had plans,' Evans said.

'Did it involve drink and women?' Stewart asked.

Evans hesitated. 'My mother's been taken ill.'

'If she's hammered back as much booze as you have, I can see why. Would you like to take some time off?'

'I wouldn't mind, sir.'

'I bet you fucking wouldn't. You've just had six weeks off. Get your arse up to the Cairngorms. They have booze up there, but if I get a report you've been out on the lash, getting pished and tossing your bag in public, well, you know what will happen.' Stewart flicked his lighter a few times.

'Yes, sir. Be my pleasure to accompany DCI Dunbar.'

'Good. Now fuck off, and make sure you tell that

twat in uniform about me parting his hair with my lighter.'

'Will do. Hopefully, if he's a smoker, he'll have his own.'

'Oh, by the way,' Stewart said, 'a uniform came in here a wee while ago and I was eavesdropping. He was talking about Linda Fry. Any of you bastards seen her recently? I'm sure she nicked my watch years ago.'

'I haven't seen her in a long time,' Dunbar said.

'Well, somebody has,' Stewart said. 'Manky bastard. Must be desperate.' He looked at Evans. 'I know a young laddie like you wouldn't touch her. Especially since you've been fucking milking your time off with a broken ankle. You know, when I was in the army, we could run ten miles with a broken ankle and still make it back to the barracks in time for our tea. Fucking young ones nowadays.'

Dunbar and Evans stood up and they left the office.

'Hobson's choice, eh, son?' said Dunbar. 'Stay here and entertain the station mascot or come with me up north. Either way, fun will be had by all.'

'Scruffy bastard?' Evans said. 'This is a designer beard.'

'Pish.'

A man wearing overalls walked into the incident room and knocked on the office door. He went in and didn't close the door all the way. They heard muted voices before Stewart blew a gasket.

'How the fuck should I know who burnt the fucking blinds? Probably one of you lot, bunch of lazy bastards. Just get on with it and replace the fucking things. And no raking about in the fucking drawers either.'

Dunbar and Evans left the incident room.

'Do you think I'll get my friendship ring back?' Evans asked.

'You'll be lucky to get a discount on a fish supper after you tell her it's finished. Never mind, there's plenty more fish –'

Evans held up a hand. 'Salt in the wounds, boss.'

THREE

'It was really nice of your brother to have us over for Christmas dinner yesterday,' DS Alex Maxwell said as they drove over the Queensferry Crossing bridge. 'I like Derek. And Briony's a good cook.'

'It was good to see them again,' DCI Harry McNeil said to his wife. 'I just wish Chance had been able to get some time off.'

'Our boy will be home soon.' Alex always referred to her stepson as her boy, although there was only twelve or so years between them.

'When he called last week, he said he'd seen Jimmy and Robbie a few times. Jimmy's keeping an eye on him.'

'It would be great if he eventually got into CID.'

'He'll have to do his two years' probation first. It's only been six months, give or take.'

The road was wet and the snow grew heavier the further north they travelled as the elevation rose.

'I was looking forward to having a few jars in the bowling club tonight too. Hopefully, this case won't take too long and we can head back home for Hogmanay,' Harry said.

'Out with the old and in with the new. Not husbands, though. You're quite safe.'

Harry looked at her. 'I already knew I was. I'm priceless. One of a kind.'

'Yeah, that's what I was thinking.'

'I don't have the strength to argue. Jeni Bridge is a hard taskmaster. Boxing Day. I ask you. Just because she's on her own and doesn't like anybody else having fun.'

'Some poor woman has been murdered, let's not forget that,' Alex said. 'And let's cut Jeni some slack. She works hard to keep Edinburgh in line.'

'That's it, bring the mood down.' He closed his eyes and tried not to think of his late mother. She should have been at the Christmas table, but instead her ashes had been scattered in the cold sea at Inverness.

Derek had taken it hard. Drinks after dinner had turned into reminiscing about their mother, and one drink had led to another. Before Harry knew it, he was being poured into the back of the car. He didn't remember getting home or climbing the stairs to their flat. He'd hear all about it from Alex soon, though.

'You going to invite your folks round for a drink on New Year's?' he asked, keeping his eyes shut. If he wasn't looking out the windscreen, he wasn't about to throw up.

'Nope.'

He felt there was another *fuck 'em* coming, but she had apparently run out of expletives to use on her father. Her parents hadn't come to their wedding and Alex had been more angry than disappointed. They hadn't been in communication since, and sometimes Harry felt guilty because they thought he was wrong for their daughter. He had reached out to her parents, but her father had just shouted abuse at him. Harry had kept calm and told the old man that if he ever changed his mind, he knew where Alex was. What he had really wanted to say to him wouldn't have gone down too well.

Alex seemed lost in her own thoughts now, so he took the chance to catch up on some sleep.

The further north they went, the heavier the snow became, but the Audi took the weather in its stride.

'We're almost there,' Alex said eventually. 'I hope you didn't need a pit stop in Pitlochry after all.'

'No, I'm fine,' he lied, needing to go now but not wanting to admit that she had been right when she said that he would be desperate by the time they got to Blairgowan.

'No, you're not. I bet you're bursting right now.' She grinned at him.

'Well, you know what they say about only renting drink for a wee while.'

'Cheers for that. There's an image I won't get out of my mind.'

She slowed down for a truck and watched as somebody on a suicide mission cut out from the line of traffic and went past in a splash of snow and ice.

'Some yahoo going skiing, no doubt,' she said, leaving the main road. A *Welcome to Blairgowan* sign ushered them into the small town.

There was a large board at the side of the road advertising *Christmas Land, the best Christmas market in the world!* – followed in brackets by the word *probably*, to ward off any lawsuits, no doubt.

'I hope this place has some life in it,' Harry said, seeing a boarded-up shop.

'I'm sure they serve drink, so you boys should be okay.'

'I was thinking of colour TV.'

The satnav took them to the hotel in the centre of town. The Highland View. It was a three-story affair and looked busy. Snow covered everything except the main road, which had been sprayed with salt.

'Doesn't it look pretty?' Alex said. 'I wish we were here just to have fun.'

'I'm sure we can fit some fun in.'

Alex called Jimmy Dunbar and he told her they had parked in a small car park opposite the hotel on the other side of the road. He came out of the main door, a hooded parka on.

'Hello, sir,' she said.

'Since when did you start calling me sir?' Dunbar replied. He walked forward and looked into the car. Harry had somehow managed to doze off.

'Hi, Harry.'

'Hi, Jimmy. How was the trip north?'

'I thought that plane back in the summer was bad enough, the one we flew to the island on. But the bloody car was just as bad. I gave Robbie a carrier bag and told him if he got puke on my shoes, he'd have one inserted where only a proctologist would be able to find it.'

'Where is he?'

'He'll be ready shortly. Let's get you checked in and then we can go to this estate. It's not far. I called Muckle and told him we wouldn't be much longer. I want to see the crime scene before it gets dark.'

Harry got out of the car and got their bags from the back.

'How was Christmas?' Dunbar asked.

'Partying like it's nineteen ninety-nine. Only my body doesn't know it's twenty-twenty.'

'I hear you.'

They crossed the road and checked in. Twenty minutes later, they met up in the lobby.

Dunbar looked at his watch and then at Evans. 'Where have you been?'

'I thought I'd have a quick shave. And give myself a haircut.'

'Why don't you take time to learn the fucking bagpipes while you're at it? Anything but get ready to go to a crime scene.'

'I wasn't that long.'

Dunbar turned to Harry. 'Robbie decided that the Taliban look was too much.' He snatched the woollen cap off Evans's head. 'Baldy as well. Right down to the wood. Why didn't you show our friends from the east your new-wave man-bun?'

'It was a ponytail,' said Evans. 'But I thought I'd smarten myself up now I'm back on duty.'

'Daft bastard fell down some stairs and broke his ankle,' Dunbar told Harry. 'He's been skiving for the past six weeks. Oh, that reminds me, did you ever meet Linda Fry when you were in Glasgow?'

'I didn't meet her,' Harry said, 'but I've heard of her. Why? You thinking of leaving Cathy for her?'

'Not a chance. I'd rather live on my own with Scooby.' Dunbar gave Evans a look. 'Robbie here's looking around for a good woman. He's not got anybody on the go just now. Have you, son?'

'No. Dad.'

'Be it on your heid,' Dunbar whispered to Evans as Harry and Alex crossed over the road to the car park.

Then Dunbar looked at Evans. 'How did you manage to cut your own hair?'

'I brought my own hair clippers. I think I missed a wee bit at the back. Maybe you could help me trim it later.'

'Aye, fucking watch me.'

They followed their colleagues across the road and got into the Land Rover that Dunbar had taken from the pool.

'It was like driving a bloody truck all the way up here,' Dunbar said.

'I thought it was okay,' Evans said from the back seat.

'That's because you were sleeping most of the way. Drunken sod. He's still hungover from yesterday.'

Dunbar drove, while Alex, looking at Google Maps, directed him. Ten minutes later, they found the Blairgowan estate.

'Just like old times, eh?' Dunbar said, pulling into the large, snow-covered car park in front of the huge stone house and parking next to other vehicles. 'The four of us up at that Highland Hotel.'

A large man with a big dog was waiting for them at the front door. Sparky got excited as if he remembered them, which was better than him ripping their balls off.

'Muckle, good to see you again,' Dunbar said. 'Still not made it back to Glasgow, I see.' He bent down to pet the dog, who was wagging his tail and nuzzling him.

'Good to see you again, sir. Aye well, maybe after this gig finishes. But if you don't mind, I'll show you the crime scene first. Then we can talk.'

Muckle led the way round the house and across the huge lawn at the back. As they entered the woods, the German shepherd started to tug at his lead.

'Sparks! Easy, ya hoor. That'll look barry if I go flat on my fucking pancake again.'

'He's a good boy you've got there, Muckle,' Harry said.

'Aye, but the rooms they gave us only have single beds in them and this fat bastard takes up most of the bed.' Muckle turned to look at Dunbar. 'And I mean him, not me.'

'I've only got a wee dug and he's the same. No matter what size they are, it's *their* bed and we can only try to fit into what tiny bit they leave for us.'

'And he snores like a bastard. I don't know who's worse, him or the wife.'

They cut into the trees and followed a path.

'Harry said your pal's here working with you,' Alex said.

'Wee Shug? Aye. And we have a woman on the team too. Miss Vern. She's terrific. They're both up there now.'

'How many's on the team, Muckle?' Evans asked.

'Five of us in total during the day, two on early and three of us on the back shift because it gets busier after dark. And a couple of guys on through the night, but they're older blokes, basically just some ears and eyes to keep a watch on things and give us a shout if anybody's creeping about touching stuff. So far we haven't had a bit of bother. Until last night.'

'Is this all private land?' Dunbar asked.

'Aye. A few thousand acres. It goes all over the place. It's a popular spot at Christmas with the skiing fraternity, so they said.'

They walked up through the snow.

'How's your bare heid now without that mop on top?' Dunbar asked Evans as they fell behind a bit.

'I can't believe Harry knows Linda,' Evans replied in a hushed tone. 'I feel like a right twat.'

'Look at it this way: you both had a good time. But

you should be giving thought to settling down. Maybe get yourself hitched and have a family.'

'It's just finding the right lassie.' He shook his head. 'Fucking friendship ring.'

They saw lights on in the woods, being fed by a generator. People walking about. Dunbar's plan to get here before dark had gone sideways and darkness had jumped them when they weren't looking.

Harry saw the spot they had marked where the woman had been cut down. He and Alex approached it.

FOUR

'Whoa, whoa, fucking hell!' said a man in a forensics suit, striding over to them on the trampled snowy path, trying not to lose his balance or his dignity as his plastic suit rustled. 'This is a crime scene, chief. You can't come up here and start making a bollocks of it.'

'And you are?' Harry said.

'Listen to me and listen good. This is my crime scene, and while I'm in charge of it, you big-city slickers will just have to follow protocol.'

'We're hardly going to strip off and dance naked round a fire on it,' Dunbar said. 'What's your name, son?'

'Ewan Gibson. Lead forensics officer.'

'My name's DCI Dunbar.'

'I know who you are. And who's the mad bastard

we've been hearing about, the one who made a call to up here?'

'You're going to have to be more specific. There're a lot of us down there. But we need to look around this scene, get an idea of what we're working on.'

'Aye, just as well we're wrapping up here for now,' Gibson said. 'Or else I might have sent you packing to do a bit of sightseeing and kill time.'

'Give us a rundown on what happened,' Harry said.

'Right then. See that rope still hanging from the tree? That's where she was hanging,' Gibson said.

'You need a degree in forensics to figure that out?' Evans said.

Gibson looked at him for a moment. 'You don't want to cross swords with me. You're on my patch.' The man sneered.

To Evan's credit, he didn't rise to the bait but just looked at the scene as Dunbar shot him a *fucking shut it* look.

'There she was, hanging by her neck, when those two came upon her. Them and that big gawk with the radge dug. I warned him well not to let it piss anywhere near here. Fucking thing nearly took my hand off and I wasn't even going to touch it. I don't think either of them is all there.'

'That your professional opinion?' Harry asked.

'It's the opinion of any daft bastard who goes near the mutt.'

'He can hear you,' Muckle said.

'Can he? Good. Maybe he'll listen next time I'm shouting, *Get that fucking dug away from me.*'

'What else do you have?' Harry said.

'Right. What he did was, he put a rope over a branch, yanked her up off her feet and tied it to another tree. Her hands and feet were tied. There were footprints there, at the base of the other tree, but some snow got through the canopy of trees and messed them up a bit.'

'Anything forensics worth noting?' Dunbar asked.

'The rope is something you can get out of any do-it-yourself shop. We found a cigarette butt over by the other tree. And for the grand finale, we found some blood spots on the trail leading away up the hill. Miraculously, they weren't covered by snow, and since this is a pathway, the snow was compacted, so the spots were sitting on top and we could lift samples.'

'Blood from the girl?' Alex asked.

'No. She was hanged, but there were no external wounds. No bleeding.'

'She maybe got a smack at him or kicked him as he was hauling her up,' Evans said.

'Could be that she fought with him before he put the rope on her. We'll have it checked at the lab in

Inverness,' Gibson said to him. 'He put the rope round her neck and tightened it, then he started hauling on it from over there so he could pull her up. His face wouldn't have been near her feet when he was pulling.'

'Any identification on her?' Harry asked.

'A wallet. Name, Carol Douglas. She's a resident here. It's been bagged and put into the van. One of my assistants can get it for you.'

Two figures dressed in black were on the other side of the blue-and-white tape, a small man and a tall woman, standing beside a uniformed sergeant.

Wee Shug waved and ducked under the tape, then held it up for the woman, and they walked down the path. The sergeant stopped to talk to another uniform.

'Hi, people,' Shug said, beaming a smile when he recognised Harry and Dunbar. 'Glad you could join us. This is Vern, Miss Vern we call her.'

'What's Vern short for?' Evans asked.

'What do *you* think it's short for?'

'Vern,' Evans said in a quieter voice.

'And there we are. I would like to present this trophy for the Scottish Detective of the Year to...?' She raised her eyebrows at him.

'DCI Jimmy Dunbar,' Evans said.

'Don't listen to him, hen. *I'm* DCI Dunbar. He's DS Robbie Evans. Or *Nob* as we call him.'

'Pleased to meet you, DS Nob.' She smiled and held out a hand to him.

They shook hands and stood back when the uniformed sergeant came over to them. 'Who's lead investigator here?' he asked.

Harry nodded to Dunbar.

'DCI Dunbar. Who are you, son?'

'Sergeant Lamb. No disrespect meant, sir, but the superintendent on the phone started shouting after I suggested we could cope for a couple of days until MIT got here. He thought I was trying it on and being belligerent. Nothing could be further from the truth. You can have as much help as you need, and we're here in a support role. I don't know why he flew off the handle.'

'He's under a lot of stress. Don't worry about it,' Dunbar replied. 'Tell me what you've got going over that hill with the blood spots.'

'We followed them as far as we could, then there seemed to be a disturbance in the snow, like somebody had stepped off the path into the woods themselves, stepping in the deep snow. The blood trail stopped. If he did go through the woods, there's a car park on the other side of the hill, near the start of another hiking trail. I've sent a couple of men round.'

'Good job. Where was the body taken to?'

'Blairgowan hospital. It has a mortuary. It's very well-equipped.'

'Unusual to find a mortuary in a small place like this,' Dunbar said.

'To the casual observer, yes, but the Cairngorms provide us with a lot of patients, and the roads here would give the autobahn a run for its money. We have quite a few people who end their lives here, either on the mountain or on the roads.'

'Okay, son. I appreciate your attitude. Don't worry about Calvin Stewart. We're here to help, that's all.'

'I understand, sir.'

Dunbar walked back to Muckle. 'Does the big house have cameras?'

'No. The old man who owns the property lives in a separate wing on the east side. His daughter wanted to have cameras installed, but his answer was, they didn't have cameras back in the seventeenth century, so he's not going to spoil the look of the house now. That's what she told me.'

'We should maybe get along to the hospital, see what they have,' Harry said. The light was completely gone now and it was getting even colder.

'Good idea,' said Dunbar. 'You and Alex can go there. I'll take Robbie to see where the lassie lived. Then we'll meet up at the station.'

FIVE

The town seemed to open wider the further north they got, with civilisation being measured in how many supermarkets there were.

'Seeing that Tesco over there is making me hungry,' Harry said as Alex navigated a roundabout.

'If you're a good boy, I'll buy you a Mars Bar for later.'

'I think I'll need a real bar later. I'm thinking about the party we were supposed to be going to.'

'The bowling club will still be there when we get back.'

'Aye, I know, but it's the famous Boxing Day shindig. I haven't missed it in years.'

'There's a bar in the hotel, Harry. We could grab a pint before bed.'

'You always know the right things to say.'

St. Luke's Hospital was up on the left. It wasn't a huge affair like the Royal in Edinburgh but was still substantial, big enough to accommodate the locals from all around the area and the influx of skiers whose ambitions far exceeded their abilities.

The mortuary sign was tucked down at the bottom of the department board, sulking like a former child actor who was over the hill and now just accepted small parts.

'How would you feel living in a place like this?' Harry asked as the headlight beams from Alex's Audi cut through the car park. It was well lit and snow filled in the shadows.

A couple of ancillary trucks were parked beside a roller door. There was a sign on the other door next to it that told them they had arrived at their destination. Almost the final destination for some.

'Now we just need some boy to come nashing out from behind the industrial bins with a chainsaw and we'll have had the whole *crapping ourselves* tour,' Harry said as they got out.

'That's only for films,' Alex replied.

'Of course it is.' Harry kept looking around nonetheless while Alex fiddled with her keys.

Come on, for fuck's sake, he thought, sure he had seen a shadow creeping about over by another door. He was about to alert Alex when a kitchen worker flicked a dead cigarette away and went back through the door.

At last, Alex rang a bell at the side of the door to the mortuary. A few minutes later, a man with a bloodied axe opened it wide and took a swing at her. Harry stepped in, grabbed the axe and took it off him.

He closed his eyes for a second and when he opened them again, instead of an axe murderer, there was a young woman standing there smiling. She looked at Alex's warrant card and then looked over at Harry, and he let her read his card.

He looked at her face and was drawn to the nose piercing. He had often wondered if such a thing brought tears to the eyes.

'Come in. I have the coffee on. It would freeze the nuts off a polar bear tonight. Not that it's like the Bahamas during the day, but I like to fiddle with the thermostat now and again. We have our own temperature-controlled environment, for the guests. I'm Stacey Nichols, by the way. Should have led with that one, I suppose.'

They stepped inside, Harry wondering if the young woman had been smoking something that made her jabber on. Or maybe it was just the way up here.

'We'd like to talk about one of your recent check-ins,' Harry said, already wishing he'd remembered his little tub of chest rub to put under his nose.

'Which one?' she asked, leading them along a corridor past the receiving area. Harry looked through the reinforced glass in a door. A van sat in the middle of the bay.

'How many do you have?' Alex asked.

'Three today alone. We had four in storage. Two skiing accidents and a car crash. We really should have a pamphlet made up and put in hotel rooms with our photo on the front. Maybe alongside a photo of the mountains above. Sort of before and after pictures. With the advertising slogan, *Drive like an arse and this is where we're going to put you: into a fridge.*'

Harry thought the tourist board had dodged a bullet when Stacey decided her future was in the mortuary and not promoting Scotland.

'It's the female. Hanging,' Harry said. Already he was getting the heebie jeebies from the antiseptic smell. Why in God's name had Dunbar asked him to come here?

'Ah, yes, young Carol. So sad. I'll take you through to speak with the doc. She'll be able to tell you more.'

Through a door and along another corridor to the office. Stacey knocked on the door and the older woman behind the desk looked up. 'Jesus, Stacey, maybe whistle, or scrape your foot on the floor, or even give us a chorus of "Oh What a Beautiful Morning".'

Stacey raised her eyebrows. 'I'll bring the Blair-gowan pipe band next time. Feardy pants.'

'I am not feardy pants, thank you. I am, however, older than you and therefore my arteries have had a lot longer to harden. I'd rather not book a fridge drawer just yet.'

Stacey smiled. 'I hardly think you've got one foot in the grave.' She gestured to the two detectives. 'DCI Harry McNeil and DS Alex Maxwell, for your pleasure, ma'am. Officers, this is our esteemed leader, Dr Valerie Henderson. They're here for the hanging.' She made it sound like a spectator sport.

'Sit down,' Valerie said. 'Stacey, be a love and grab us some coffee.'

'Will do.'

'Not for me,' Harry said, not wanting to puke in here; the coffee would add to an already tumultuous stomach.

'I'm fine,' Alex said.

'Just you and me, boss. Be right back.'

Stacey left and Valerie rubbed the bridge of her nose. 'It's always the damn eyes that get me first – tired, dry. And then the headaches. I need a good break, but that's not going to happen anytime soon. We get a little lull when the skiing season finishes, but then the hikers take over. More often than not, one of them falls down a ravine, or they go swimming in the nice, calm water, which is freezing, and drown. You wouldn't believe the deaths up here. After a while, they stop becoming headlines and are just part of society.'

The detectives sat and looked at her, waiting for her to finish.

She smiled. 'Sorry. Too much caffeine. I tried quitting but started getting caffeine withdrawal headaches, so I went right back to it.' She sighed. 'God, there I go again. You wanted to know about Carol?'

'We do,' Harry said, deciding to jump in now while Valerie had stopped to take a breath.

'She was a nice young woman. In and out of hospital for many years. I thought she was getting better, but it seems not. To take her own life by that means is sad.'

'She was murdered,' Alex said.

'What? Are you sure?'

'Yes. We had forensics go over the scene and she couldn't have killed herself given the way the rope was. We can't go into too much detail, but we wanted to talk to you about the post-mortem.'

Valerie looked shocked for a moment. 'I haven't started it yet. I just finished a skier. Carol's booked for tomorrow morning. Oh my God. Dudley will be so upset.'

'Dudley?' Harry asked.

'Matthews. He was her therapist. He works upstairs.'

'Did he discuss Carol with you?'

'Oh, no, of course not. Not in the way you're implying. But Carol was a local. We all knew her. Everybody knows *of* her.'

'She's well known around here?' Alex asked.

'Not a celebrity, but she's known as the survivor.'

'What does that mean?'

'Six years ago, three girls were abducted, one after the other. She was the only one who made it back alive.'

SIX

Dudley Matthews was a tall, skinny man – in his fifties, if Harry were to hazard a guess. A beanpole, some people might call him, although the man had a bit of a beer gut on him. Harry didn't blame the man for drinking. It was a hazard of the job, one with which he was all too familiar. He had seen many men being gripped by the bottle, unable to let go until their life was turned upside down.

'Please, sit down. Thank you for coming to see me and letting me know about Carol.'

They sat down in comfortable chairs in his office. The heat was seeping into Harry, leading him towards dozing off, so he loosened his tie.

'We believe she was a patient of yours,' Alex said.

'Yes, but you understand, even though she's dead, there's still confidentiality.'

'Oh, yes, we understand that Doctor,' Harry said. 'We were thinking more along the lines of you being able to think of somebody who might want to harm Carol.'

'Without breaking confidentiality,' Matthews said again, as if fearing the detectives were trying to trap him, 'there was no mention of anybody who would harm her.'

'It's public knowledge that Carol went missing along with two other girls six years ago. Can you shed some more light on that?'

'Of course. As it's something that was in the papers, then yes, I'd be happy to go over that with you.' Matthews was looking at them like they were playing poker and he was wondering how his poker face looked.

'Yes, it was a bad time for us all. Two girls were abducted, months apart. They were missing for a few days before they were found hanged in the woods. Carol was the third one, but she fought him and escaped. "A man with a beard" was the best description she could give. And this was all in the papers, by the way.'

'We understand,' said Harry. 'I'll read the report later. We just wanted to hear a local's point of view.'

'There are a lot of people here in the town all year round. Hikers in the summer, skiers in the winter.

People passing through, stopping for a bite to eat on their way up north. That sort of thing. A stranger doesn't stand out.'

Matthews looked down at his lap for a moment. 'But there's one last thing that made it murder.' He had Harry and Alex's undivided attention. 'There were sleeping tablets in the first girl's system. Made it easier to transport her to the woods.'

'That does sound like the kicker right there,' Harry had to admit. 'Who found her?'

'A boy out walking his dog.'

'What about the second murder?'

'Summer 2014. Three months after the first murder. A teenage girl out walking her dog along one of the trails. She didn't turn up for dinner and the parents started getting worried. They called their daughter's friends. Nothing. Then somebody found her dog, a little Scottie. He had blood on his white coat. He was walking about trailing his lead.

'It was a week before they found her. In the woods, hanging by her neck from a tree. He'd also stabbed her. That's why her dog had blood on him.'

'She was friends with the first one?' Alex asked.

'Yes. They went to high school together. They were both friends with Martin, the boy who found the first girl.'

'Do you think he found Carol?' Harry asked. 'Witnesses saw a man running away. Could it have been him?'

Matthews took off his glasses and polished them with a small cloth. 'I don't know. Martin had a complete mental breakdown after finding the first victim. He's spent the last six years in New Craigs Psychiatric Hospital in Inverness.'

'Is he under your supervision now?'

Matthews put his glasses back on. 'He is. He's thirty now and has come back to live with his family.'

'Where do they stay?'

'They own the Blairgowan estate. His name's Martin Blair.'

SEVEN

'You're not sleeping, are you?' Jimmy Dunbar said to Robbie Evans as they turned a corner and the big car carried straight on, until Dunbar corrected the vehicle.

'No. This is my *shitting myself* face in case you haven't seen it before. Which I think you have.'

'Don't talk pish. I've driven bigger machines than this.'

'Go-karts don't count.'

'How about it, Muckle?' Dunbar looked in the rear-view mirror and saw the big man holding a grab handle with one hand and Sparky with the other.

'I think your driving's fine. Sparky thinks it's shite, though.' The dog barked in agreement.

They drove further down the road.

'Anytime you feel like jumping in, Muckle. Left, right or straight on?'

'Hang on, Jimmy, I'm trying to get my bearings,' Muckle said.

'We're the ones who should be saying that. We've only just got here. You, on the other hand, have been staying in this fucking backwater for a month now. This is not the time for getting your bearings.'

'Second left. I remember it now.'

Dunbar made the turn and the car bit in and got itself going up the hill like it was on drugs.

'All or nothing with this fucking thing. How did the army cope with them?' he said. He stopped the vehicle at the top of an incline with houses on either side.

'I feel like I should put the kettle on and make some sandwiches, we've got that much time. You lost your marbles again there, son?'

'Bearings,' Muckle corrected.

'I think I was right first time.'

'There it is.' He pointed across the road and along to the right. 'That's the house we're looking for.'

'You sure now? I mean, it's no' halfway up Ben Nevis or something?'

'Wrong part of the country.'

Dunbar drove into the street and stopped half on, half off the pavement outside a house. The heavy snow was making it difficult to distinguish what was what.

'I'll stay in the motor here, Jimmy,' Muckle said.

'Aye, you do that, son. I'll give you a shout if we need Sparky boy there.'

Dunbar and Evans played games with the gate, which didn't want to shove the snow out of the way. Dunbar eventually got it open far enough to get through and they made their way to the front door.

'Notice how I wouldn't have had to open the gate so far?' Evans said.

'So I'm a fat bastard now?'

'I'm kidding, boss.'

'Maybe it's all those fish suppers I've been eating. But tell you what, I think I'll start using the one along the road. You know, the one where what's-her-name works?'

'Actually, I meant to ask, you been working out?' Evans said, reaching around his boss and ringing the doorbell.

'Too late now, cheeky bastard.'

A young female family liaison officer answered the door. Dunbar and Evans showed their warrant cards.

'We need to talk to the family,' Dunbar said.

She smiled and stepped aside. 'I was just about to get the kettle on.'

'Where's your patrol car?'

'We don't have that many to go around. I was dropped off. Mr Douglas is in the living room, on your left. Mrs Douglas is in bed. She was sedated by the doctor.'

They wiped their feet on a mat before going in. The thermostat was at the right temperature, not making the house seem like it was on fire.

'Mr Douglas? DCI Dunbar. DS Evans. We're heading up the investigation into the murder of your daughter. I'd like to ask some questions.'

Douglas sighed and pointed to the couch. The TV was on, but it had been muted. 'Aye, fire away, son.'

Douglas looked to be in his late forties, but his red eyes made him appear older.

They sat down and Dunbar looked at him. 'First of all, we're sorry for your loss, and although I can't promise you the earth, I can promise you we'll do everything in our power to find the culprit.'

'I know you will. But I don't think you have to look far, do you?'

'I'm sorry, do you have a name for us?'

Douglas drew his attention away from the TV to look at Dunbar. 'That psycho nut-job who just got released from the loony bin. Martin Blair. You should check him out. He found one of the lassies hanging from the tree six years ago. The first one. He could have been at the scene of the second one, who knows? They found her after a search when her wee dog was found. Exactly the same spot, three months apart.'

'Did this Martin bloke know the girls?'

'He did. He was their friend. In a place like this, friends are cherished. There's a lot of interlopers, so the locals stick together more than they would in a big city.'

'Did they have a falling-out with him?' Evans asked. 'I mean, did Carol ever mention anything?'

Douglas curled his bottom lip up and shook his head. 'Far from it. They protected Martin. Some of those bastards at the school mocked him, saying he was daft, and it was true, he did have learning difficulties. But he had the protection of his family, so the bullying only went so far. Any kid caught doing it was expelled right away.'

'What makes you think Martin had something to do with Carol's death?' Dunbar asked.

'Just something Carol said the day before she died. She said to me, "Dad, I'm scared. Martin's out of the hospital."' Douglas looked at both men. 'She didn't elaborate. Before that, she'd always spoken about Martin like he was her friend, but when she learned of his release, that seemed to change her mind.'

'How old was Carol?'

'Just turned twenty. She was fourteen when the other two girls were murdered.'

'Back then, did the police have any suspects?' Evans asked.

'No.'

'Was Martin suspected?'

'No. Not really. I mean, they questioned him, of course, but he's one cucumber short of a sandwich, and his grandfather put the brakes on pretty sharpish. Then the boy had a breakdown and they took him away.'

'How long has Martin been out of the hospital?' Dunbar asked.

'Not sure. Maybe a few weeks.'

Dunbar stood up. 'If you think of anything else, Mr Douglas, then please call us. We can be reached at the station or you can call my mobile number.' He handed the man a business card.

Outside, it looked like they had been transported to the Arctic Circle. The FLO didn't waste much time in closing the door behind them.

Back at the car, Sparky looked up and wagged his tail as Dunbar got back in the big vehicle. The heat was welcoming.

'Muckle, you said you saw somebody hanging around where the lassie was hanging, then he ran off. You said he had a beard.'

'Aye.'

'Could it have been a young man with a ski mask on or something?'

Muckle shook his head. 'No, it was definitely a

beard. I shone my light on his face. It was an older bloke. Why?'

Dunbar told him about Martin.

'I speak to the laddie all the time. He walks with a limp, the result of a fall when he was little. This guy took off like his arse was on fire. It wasn't Martin.'

'Then who the hell was it?'

EIGHT

The police station was a modern, two-storey affair that could have passed for any business if it weren't for the Police Scotland sign outside the front door. Inside, the heat was pumping out, warming bones that had been chilled by the snow.

Jimmy Dunbar stood at the whiteboard while the others sat on chairs. There were a few uniforms in and they stood around the periphery.

'Thanks for being here and lending us your station,' Dunbar said, more to keep the peace than anything else – it didn't do any harm to have the locals on his side. 'My colleagues went to speak with Dr Dudley Matthews over at the hospital. You probably all know him, but it was my first time meeting with him. He gave us the rundown on Martin Blair. Who here knows him?'

All the locals' hands shot up.

The sergeant spoke up: 'The Blair family have been around here for generations. They started the town really. Built up the tourism. They're well-respected round here.'

'Nobody's here to dance on anybody's toes, son. But we're going to have a talk with Martin Blair, just because of his connection to the past cases from six years ago. Anybody here work those cases, where the two young lassies went missing?'

One or two hands didn't go up.

'Right, we had the rundown from Matthews, so we know pretty much what went on back then. Martin found the first one, but the second victim was discovered after her little dog was found running about in the town with blood on him. A search party found her in the same woods, hanging from a tree.

'Young Martin Blair had a mental breakdown and was admitted to the psychiatric hospital. Now he's back, only been released for a short time. And now there's another lassie been murdered.'

Dunbar turned to face them all. 'I want to know the whereabouts of Blair. I don't care if his family are the richest people in town or not, we need to talk to him. I know Christmas Land sits on his property, but if they object, we'll get him in here. Any questions?'

Sergeant Lamb put his hand up. 'Any word on the

man who was seen running away from the last murder scene?'

'Nothing yet. "A man with a beard" doesn't exactly narrow it down. Did your uniforms get anything from the car park on the other side of the trail?' Dunbar said.

'Nothing, sir. There was evidence that cars had been there earlier in the day, but the tyre tracks were being filled in by snow.'

'If he left on foot, where would he have gone?'

'The car park is off a little road. He could have walked down and into the town in ten minutes. Nobody would have blinked an eye, there are so many strangers going about.'

'Okay. I want background checks on the three girls who were killed. I want everything there is to know about them.' Dunbar looked at his watch. 'It's late. Let's meet up here first thing tomorrow. But Sergeant Lamb, I'd like you to get a couple of uniforms to patrol round Christmas Land tonight. They have security, but I'd rather they had backup.'

'Yes, sir.'

Dunbar walked over to Harry, Alex and Evans. 'We should grab some dinner.'

'I thought I'd have a walk round Christmas Land, if you don't mind, sir,' Evans said.

'Aye, off you go. Tell Muckle what's going on. We'll drop you off.'

They left the small incident room.

NINE

The big police vehicle got them through the heavy snow, which was beginning to come down harder by the time they got to the Blairgowan estate. They pulled into the car park and a car that had been following them carried on down towards the Christmas Land car park, on a separate road.

'Anybody could come in here by car and nobody would bat an eye,' Harry said. 'I don't understand why they don't have cameras, even if they were discreet ones.'

'People with money are tight bastards,' Dunbar said. 'They can afford the big stuff because they cheap out on the small stuff.'

They watched as a Subaru estate car pulled in beside them and they turned to look at the driver.

Shug came out of the big house just as they were piling out of the Land Rover.

'You're just in time,' Shug said to them, squinting his eyes against the driving snow.

'For what?' Alex asked.

He smiled as the driver got out of the Subaru. 'This is David, my husband. David, meet the crew from Edinburgh and Glasgow: Harry, Jimmy, Alex and Robbie.'

'Howdy, folks,' David said, lifting a hand. He was a tall man, thin, with glasses. He reminded Dunbar of Dudley Matthews and he briefly wondered if they were related.

David reached into the car and pulled out a brown paper bag and handed it to Shug. 'You left it on the counter,' he said. He had a posh English accent.

'Come on, let's get inside,' Shug said.

'Is Christmas Land still open?' Evans asked.

'It is. A little snow doesn't stop the visitors.'

'Is...Muckle down there? Do you take a break on shifts, or...'

'Vern's inside having a coffee with Muckle. We have a quick meal break. We have radios in case the big riot of 2020 kicks off. Why don't we all go in and have something to eat? There's plenty to go round.'

'Lead the way, son. I could eat a scabby horse,'

Dunbar said. Shug wondered if people talking about eating horses was a Glaswegian thing.

They all went into the big house and through a doorway next to the side of the large staircase. The corridor led down to the kitchen at the back of the house.

'This house is full of wee passageways,' Shug explained. 'The new wing was built on the other side of the house. I say new, but it was built in the sixties.'

They went into the kitchen, where Muckle was sitting at a table talking to Vern.

'I hope you left us some scran,' Shug said.

'There's a ton of it,' said Muckle. 'Even the dug's had his fill. I'll be lucky if he wants to go back out now. Look at him. He's got his *I've just farted* grin on.'

'Oh, leave him alone,' Vern said, and Sparky lifted his head and gave his tail a quick wag. He didn't detect a threat from the others, so he lay back down, ready to jump into action should food or trouble be presented.

Vern stood up and walked over to Evans. 'Hi, Robbie. I'm just going to pour a coffee. Want one?'

'Cheers, that would be smashing.'

She walked away, over to a big contraption that wouldn't have looked out of place in *The War of the Worlds*, and got two cups of coffee out of it.

'She's nice,' Dunbar said, standing close to Evans and lowering his voice.

'Aye, she is. Nice lassie.'

'Better than the old boiler you've been seeing.'

'Oh, aye. I thought you said your lips were sealed, but then you go and bring up Linda's name to Harry. I thought you were going to be discreet?'

'That was me being discreet. Me *not* being discreet would be to get a plane to pull a banner behind it saying, *Robbie Evans is shagging Linda Fry.*'

'You're shagging Linda Fry?' Harry said, stopping behind Dunbar.

'Naw, he's no' shagging anybody. I'm just winding him up, Harry. These young lads wouldn't know what to do with Linda.' Dunbar grinned.

'Isn't that the truth.' Harry walked away.

'Just kill me now,' Evans said.

'Relax. Harry's a good guy. Even if he did find out, he wouldn't say anything. But here's Vern. She looks interested in you, so try not to fuck this one up. Thank God you got rid of the funny wee ponytail you had.'

'You wouldn't understand. It's different from your younger days when you had to look in *The Victorian Guide to Hairstyles*.' Evans smiled as Vern approached.

'Plane. Banner,' Dunbar said.

'There you go, Robbie,' she said, handing him a mug of coffee.

'Thanks, Vern.'

Dunbar walked away and turned behind Vern's back, pointing his fingers at his eyes and then at Evans.

'Listen, I let my sense of humour get away from me today. I apologise if I offended you. It was meant to be a joke,' Vern said.

'Don't worry about it. I'll just write your name on the toilet wall.'

'Oh no, please don't. I'll get fired and they'll lock me up upstairs.'

'I was just kidding,' Evans said, his cheeks starting to burn.

Vern laughed. 'I'm just pulling your leg.' She put a hand on his arm.

'Oh, I knew that.'

'My last boyfriend called it quits with me. He didn't have a sense of humour at all. He was a nightmare. How about you? Your significant other have a sense of humour?'

Evans thought of Linda Fry and thought she definitely had been having a laugh with him. At his expense.

'No. I don't have a significant other at the moment.'

That's it, Robbie, do the wee dance there, subtly asking each other if you're available, Dunbar thought, eavesdropping on the couple. Then he left them to it.

David was tucking into a turkey sandwich and

drinking some coffee at a counter while chatting with Alex.

'David was just telling me he works in IT but from home,' Alex said.

'Ah, you're a computer geek?' Dunbar said.

'For want of a better word. I usually call myself a nerd.'

'Didn't know there was a difference.'

'One is a person who sits at a computer all day doing work on it. The other is somebody who plays games on it all day.'

'Is that right?'

David grinned and pushed his glasses up his nose. 'No. I'm just talking what you Scotch guys call pish.'

'Pulling my fucking chain and I've not even had something to eat yet.'

'Seriously, though, I work from home doing computer work for an IT security company. That's how I met Shug. We've been together for three years now.'

'I didn't meet you when we were working on the island back in the summer,' Alex said.

'No, I was doing a job that meant I had to do a bit of travelling for a few weeks. But now we've rented a house for the season and we leave January first. We're going to Glasgow after this. I can go wherever Shug gets a job.'

'That's a lot of moving about,' Dunbar said. 'I heard about Shug getting homophobic slurs at the police station.'

'Yeah, there are ignorant bastards everywhere. We're thick-skinned, though.'

'Good for you, son.'

'Maybe I could pick your brains sometime,' David said.

'About what?'

'This case. In my spare time, I write true crime books. When Shug told me about the hanged girl, that got my radar going. Then I did a little online search and found out about the other two girls who were murdered here six years ago. I'm looking into it to see if it may be worth doing a book on it.'

'Sure, anytime, pal. But you have to understand, there are some things that have to remain confidential, so we can't talk about everything.'

'Oh, I understand. Just any snippets of info you could throw my way.'

'Let us get this investigation started properly and we can all sit down and have a chinwag,' Dunbar said.

'Sorry, I have to go,' Alex said and ran out of the kitchen.

'What's wrong?' Harry said.

'Haven't any idea. She just darted out,' Dunbar said.

Harry ran out after her and found her outside in the car park, heaving into a snow-covered bush.

'Jesus, Alex, are you okay?'

'Do I look like I'm fucking okay?' she said, straightening up and wiping her eyes and her mouth. Then she heaved again.

'Too much turkey?' Harry asked.

'Too much sex,' she replied. 'I'm pregnant.'

TEN

Old Man Blair lived in the new wing on his own. He had staff to cater to his every whim, but he was a widower who wanted privacy. Tonight, his privacy was going to be disturbed.

While Dunbar didn't exactly have to peel Evans off Vern, he was giving serious consideration to throwing a bucket of water over him.

'There's no stopping you when you get going, is there?' Dunbar said. 'How about you clear some space on the dining table?'

'She's nice. I feel a connection there.'

'There you go with the fucking connection lark again. How about your arse feels a connection with my boot?'

'At least she's my age.'

'Great. Stop with the New Age hippie pish.

Connections. Just relax and be yourself. Or rather, be like me.'

'Daft in the heid?'

'Witty and charming, ya cheeky bastard. Come on, let's go and speak to the old man. Get a feel for this place.'

Dunbar waved Muckle over. Sparky stood next to Dunbar, waiting for his ears to be scratched.

'I'm assuming the old boy who lives here has staff?'

'He does, aye. He lives on his own in the wing, while his daughter and grandson live in the main house.'

'Give one of them a shout, will you. I'd like to speak to Old Man Blair. And the laddie Martin, if he's kicking around.'

'He'll be down at the market. He's always hanging about down there. One of his old friends works there, a lassie from the town.'

'I'll start with the old man. Who else lives here?'

'Martin and his mother. The staff. That's it.'

'Can you get word to the old man that we'd like a chat?'

'Aye. I'll call his personal assistant. She's a nice lassie. The old boy likes to think this is the Playboy Mansion, only without the women. Or any sense of style.'

'Go give her a call now, son.'

Muckle took Sparky away and left the huge kitchen. Dunbar took his phone out and called Harry.

'I'm going to talk to the old boy who owns this place. You in?'

'Alex has been taken ill. Can you manage that without me?'

'Of course I can manage it. That was an FYI. How's Alex?'

'She started throwing up. Must have been all the turkey.'

'Give us a shout in the morning, and if she's not feeling up to it, then she can have a lie-in. Don't be pushing her to go out and about.'

'I won't. She's resting now.'

'Stay safe.' Dunbar hung up with a feeling in his gut that it was more than turkey that was bothering Alex. Never mind, Harry would tell him in due course if it was anything else.

They left by a different door to the one they had come through and entered a formal dining room that was big enough to feed all the king's horses. Then through another door.

Muckle met Dunbar and Evans in the big entrance hallway. 'Mr Blair's a very private man, but somebody will come down and speak with you in the library.'

'Where's Vern gone?' Evans asked him.

'She's needed down at the market. I'm going there

now with the big boy. Some rowdy bastard is pished and starting to cause trouble. Call me if you need anything else.'

He walked away, Sparky starting to pull on his lead, sensing he was going back to work. 'I swear to God, if I go on my fucking arse again…'

'I wish Muckle would come back to the force,' Dunbar said. 'We need guys like him.'

'Aye, they had their chance, though,' said Evans. 'They let him go.'

A young woman came down the stairs, dressed smart-casual. Dunbar had pictured some old frump in jodhpurs for some reason.

'Officers?' she said, smiling at them.

'That would be us,' Dunbar said.

'If you'd like to follow me to the library.'

Both men followed her down another hallway and into the library. It was filled with shelves but the books weren't the traditional choice.

'Mr Blair likes to read thrillers and crime novels,' the woman said.

'You would be, ma'am?' Dunbar said.

'Oh, I'm sorry. I thought you knew everybody who worked here. Ainslie Ashworth. I'm Mr Blair's personal assistant.' The smile dropped from her face. 'Isn't it a terrible thing that happened to that poor girl?'

'It is indeed. That's why we're here, to try to catch whoever did it.'

'It's like history repeating itself, what with the other two murders.'

'Did you work here at the time?' Dunbar said, moving closer to the open fire, which had logs burning in it. He thought it strange that this big room would have a real fire going although there was nobody in it.

'No. I only started a year ago. Word is, he can't keep his assistants. Apparently, I'm going to get a long-service medal. I'm hanging in there, but it's hard. I think New Year's Day will be my last day here.'

'I don't blame you,' Evans said. 'There are plenty of bosses who are a pain.'

'Do you get any light aircraft flying overhead?' Dunbar asked Ainslie. 'Even ones pulling banners behind them?'

'No, I can't say we do.'

'First time for everything.'

'To be honest, I wish you policemen were staying here at the house. There's been some funny goings-on recently.'

'Tell me more.'

Ainslie looked nervously at the door, then back at the two men. 'I don't want to speak out of turn, but after dark, when everything is quiet, there's been a lot of arguing.'

'Between who?'

'Mr Blair and somebody else. I don't know who. But it's scary.'

Just then, Old Man Blair walked in, all smiles, wearing a smoking jacket and a cravat, as if he was carrying the Hugh Hefner look too far.

'Somebody talking about me?' Blair said. 'My ears are burning.'

'Only good things,' Dunbar said. 'Miss Ashworth here was telling us how we should visit the Christmas markets you have going.'

'You should. You can go now,' Blair said, keeping his smile in place while he nodded for Ainslie to depart.

He watched her retreat, waiting for the door to close behind her before turning back to the two detectives. 'Nice but a little dim. Please, sit down.'

Dunbar looked at Evans like he couldn't believe what he had just heard.

'Would you like a drink, boys? Something to warm the cockles?'

'We're fine, thanks,' Dunbar said as he and Evans sat down across from the old man. 'What we would like is to talk to your staff. See if they heard anything last night.'

'Oh, you mean the wee lassie who hanged herself in the woods?'

'She didn't hang herself,' Evans said. 'Somebody did that for her.'

'I can assure you that Carol didn't hang herself, Mr Blair,' Dunbar said.

'If you say so.'

'I do. She was murdered, plain and simple. That's why we need to hear from anybody who might have heard something.'

'These walls are thick. They tend to keep their secrets.' Blair smiled at Dunbar, but there was no humour there.

'What is it about the woods behind your house? Why do young girls die there?'

Blair lifted his hands. 'Young girls die every day. It just so happens that one died in the woods on my property.'

'But it wasn't just one, was it, Mr Blair?' Evans said. 'It's three now. Including the one your grandson found.'

Blair lowered his head for a moment. 'It was a shock for young Martin, right enough. Those two girls were his friends. He didn't make friends much, but those girls took him under their wing. It came as a shock to him when they were murdered.'

'He's thirty. Six years ago, he was twenty-four. They were fifteen. Some people might think that strange.'

'He's not a bloody paedo, Dunbar! He's simple.'

'Big and strong too,' Evans added.

'He thinks like a young boy. When he reached a certain age, he stopped growing mentally.'

'We heard about him ending up in the hospital,' Dunbar said. 'And now he's back.'

Blair looked at him. 'Yes, he's back, and already the fingers are pointing. Martin the loony is back in town – lock up your daughters.'

'Have you ever seen a man with a beard creeping about in the woods?' Evans said.

Blair gave him a look as if questioning his sanity. 'People hike in those woods. There are plenty of strange men with beards going about.'

'Your head of security and two others saw a bearded man running away from the scene,' Dunbar said.

Blair smiled. 'Martin doesn't have a beard. Sorry to disappoint you. He also walks with a limp. He's disabled, and I don't think he's into cross-country running.'

'What does he do with his spare time?'

'Helps out at one of the market stalls. He likes the lassie who runs it. She likes his company too, so it keeps him...'

'Out of mischief?'

'Occupied. He doesn't need to get a job for the

money, of course, but a young mind like his is fragile. It took a lot of therapy to get him on the straight and narrow again. He still goes to therapy now.'

'What about his mother?' Evans asked.

'What about her? You surely don't think she went into the woods and killed those lassies, do you?'

'Nothing's beyond the realms,' Dunbar said.

'She's in a fucking wheelchair, man!' Blair suddenly shouted, jumping to his feet. 'Now, if you want to know if I went creeping about in those woods, you'll need to ask me through a lawyer. Goodnight, gentlemen.'

The detectives stood up. 'We'll be seeing you around, Mr Blair.'

The old man stormed out of the room, leaving them standing there.

ELEVEN

Then they heard him shouting outside the door.

'No, I don't fucking need anything from you!'

A woman came in through the open doorway, pushing the wheels of her chair. 'I apologise for my father, gentlemen. Please, stay and have a drink.'

'No, thank you,' Dunbar said.

'Marjorie Blair. I told my dad to wait for me, but the little lift they put in for me sometimes doesn't want to work. He's very impulsive. I hope he wasn't too rude to you.'

'We've heard worse.'

'Please, sit. I'd be happy to answer any of your questions.'

Dunbar looked at Evans before sitting back down.

Marjorie wheeled herself closer. 'It was tragic what happened to Carol. Martin's devastated. She was one of his friends, and they had met up shortly after he got out. You know, there were fingers pointed at Martin when Chloe was murdered, and they hauled him in, questioned him like he was some kind of monster. He found her, that was it.' She looked down at her wheelchair for a moment before looking back at the two men, tears in her eyes.

'He's nothing but a boy at heart. The psychologists think he has a mental age of ten. Thereabouts. Who knows for sure?'

'Your father said Martin walks with a limp and that he's disabled,' Dunbar said.

'Just a slight limp. The way my dad describes it, Martin walks with one leg hanging off. It's just from an old injury he got years back. He fell, badly breaking his leg, and it didn't set properly. If you weren't looking for it, you wouldn't notice it.'

'He was cleared of involvement in Chloe's murder, wasn't he?' Evans said.

'Yes. They estimated the time of death and Martin was at a workshop at the time. Plenty of witnesses. Same for when Sarah was murdered three months later, but it didn't stop the vultures rounding on him, even though he didn't find her. He only found Chloe. He was supposed to meet her later that day. He had a complete meltdown after Sarah. That's why he was in the hospital. He sees Dr Matthews now.'

'How does he spend his days when he's not in therapy?' Dunbar asked.

'Right now he's spending time down at the market. Christmas Land is a godsend for him. He gets to be around people who don't judge him.'

'That's good. Everybody needs a friend.' Dunbar hesitated for a second before diving in. 'Can I ask if you have a partner?'

Marjorie smiled at him. 'I'm hardly the catch of the year. I'm forty-six and in a wheelchair. With a son some people might call retarded.'

'Forty-six?' Dunbar said.

'Yes. I had Martin when I was sixteen. Even coming from a family with money doesn't stop you doing stupid things. But I wouldn't swap Martin for the world. I'm just thankful for what we have here. There are a lot of people who have it way worse than I have, so I don't moan about it.'

'You have a good attitude, if you don't mind me saying.'

'Not at all. I just hope that helps clear some things up. In case you were wondering if Martin had killed Carol.'

'It does.'

'It's not as if Martin would be able to comprehend what you were asking him. But if there's anything else you need, just ask.'

'I'll have some uniforms talk to the rest of the people who live in the house here.'

'Just let us know and they'll be available.' She turned the chair round and rolled out of the room.

Dunbar and Evans stood up just as Ainslie came back into the room. 'I can show you out if you like,' she said.

'What do you think of Martin?' Dunbar asked.

Her cheeks grew flushed, and not from the heat in the room. 'I find him creepy, to be honest. When he sees me, he just stares. That's why I'm leaving.'

'Has he ever done anything inappropriate to you?' Evans asked.

'No, but one night I had been working late, and when I came downstairs, I saw him standing at the top, just out of sight. Another night, I looked out of my bedroom window with the light off and saw him running over the back lawn into the woods. He's just creepy.'

'But not last night?'

'I didn't see him last night at all. I heard screaming, and next thing, the security team were running across the back lawn through the snow.'

'You've been very helpful, Miss Ashworth,' Dunbar said.

The three of them left the library.

'What do you make of this Martin?' Dunbar asked Evans when they were outside.

'I think he's a creepy bastard who's more switched on than people think. We should look into him more.'

'Try to find out who his father is and if he's still around.'

'Better not ask the old boy. He looks like he takes a dive off the deep end without much of a push.'

'Aye, you're right. But take the rest of the night off,' Dunbar said. 'I'm going to FaceTime Cathy. Catch you in the morning. Get Vern to give you a lift back to the hotel. But none of your bloody shenanigans.'

'As if.'

TWELVE

Alex was sitting with a cold, wet facecloth on her forehead. 'I'm sorry you had to find out that way, honey. I'd planned so many ways to tell you in my head. In the bowling club. In the pub. Over a nice, romantic meal.'

'Instead, you waited until we came up to the Highlands of Scotland and spewed into a bush.' Harry was sitting on the bed, smiling. 'That's how I'm going to tell this story for the rest of my life.'

'Not very romantic, is it?'

'I think it is.'

'You're just saying that to get me into bed.'

'Into bed so you can rest. In case you didn't know, puking your ring into a bush isn't a turn-on. Just for future reference.'

'What will Jimmy think if I can't carry on? Christ,

I'm going to do the best I can, but right now I feel godawful.'

'I don't think Jimmy is going to mind.' Harry got off the bed and took a bottle of water from the nightstand and poured Alex a glass. 'Better stay hydrated.'

'Thanks, but I think I need to go again.' She got up from the chair where she was sitting and rushed into the bathroom. Harry switched the TV on to cover the sounds she was making.

Mortuaries and puking. Two things that turned his stomach. But the bigger picture here was his imminent entrance into fatherhood again. Chance would be eighteen next year and now Harry was going to be a dad again in his forties.

He knew it was something he wanted with Alex, but now that it was happening, he felt nervous. Would he still be a good dad to his newborn? Would the kid end up being bullied at school because Harry was older than some other kid's grandfather?

He turned the volume up as Alex went in for round two. *Jesus Christ.* He knew he should be in there, saying soothing things to her, rubbing her back, holding her. But the very sight of her being sick would make him vomit.

What about when a baby was sick? That was different. Something in the lizard brain kicked in and you stepped up. But this...he wasn't built for this. His first wife had been a regular visitor to the porcelain shrine because she was a drinker, and although Harry knew this wasn't because of the drink, he still couldn't be the knight in shining armour.

There was a light rap at the door. Harry looked through the peephole and saw it was Dunbar.

'I just thought I'd see how Alex was doing,' Dunbar said. 'I won't come in.' They both heard Alex retching. 'Jesus. I had some prawn cocktail once in a hotel in Spain that had my heid down the fucking pan for days, but it didn't sound anything like that.'

'Well, thanks for that image there, Jimmy. Now that you've ruined my appetite for breakfast, I'll pass on your good wishes to the wife.'

Dunbar grinned. 'Better get used to the puking and shitting, son. It takes a while until they're potty-trained.' He winked and walked away.

'I'll see you at breakfast,' Harry said, closing the door gently.

Then he winced when Alex went at it again. 'Fuck me.'

It was going to be a lot sooner than breakfast that he saw Dunbar again.

THIRTEEN

'That's all we fucking need, some nutter on the loose,' PC Alan Davidson said, turning the patrol car round in the snow-covered car park.

'What are we doing in here?' said his partner, PC Stan Winston.

'I need a slash. Been drinking coffee all day, but it goes right through me. Keep a shotty.'

'We're hardly in the middle of a bloody ski slope. Nobody's going to see your wee tadger flapping about in the cold oot here. Just get on with it and shut the fucking door.'

'Hey, it's only wee 'cause it's cold.'

'Hurry up, ya bawbag. Yer letting all the heat oot.'

Davidson went across to the edge of the car park, trudging through the heavy snow, until he got to the start of a hikers' pathway. What daft bastard wanted to go trudging up and down hills when they could be like him, sitting in front of the TV, drinking a tinny and getting wired into a couple of Scotch pies on rolls?

'Christ, you're making yourself hungry, Ali boy,' he told himself, moving his kit out of the way in an attempt to find his zipper. It was getting harder as each year passed. He had flipped through Amazon online looking at treadmills and broken out in a sweat looking at the prices. The decent ones were expensive. The cheapo ones made in huts by wee laddies and lassies before they went to school in some far-flung province of China were affordable, but you'd need to be prepared to take a hammer to it after it broke down a week later.

No, fuck that for a laugh. His girlfriend was just as overweight as he was. 'Let's face it, son, you're not going to be spanking any supermodels anytime soon. But that's okay. She likes to curl up on the couch just as much as you do.'

He smiled at the thought. Maybe he should ask her to marry him. She spent most of her time at his place anyway, so why not?

He didn't want to be here too long. He could imagine the headline: *Police Officer Caught Exposing Himself in Public.* That was a career-breaker if ever there was one.

He was in mid-flow when his partner leaned on the horn.

'Fuck's sake!' he shouted as his pee went down the front of his trousers. 'Aw, for God's sake.'

He turned round just in time to see a black estate car speeding past. He'd fixed himself, so even if the driver looked over, all he would see was a police officer on routine patrol.

He picked some snow up and rubbed it quickly over the front of his trousers. He would tell Winston he'd slipped and fallen; hopefully, the other man hadn't been watching him.

The big black car shot round the bend like the driver was possessed.

Davidson hurried as best he could through the snow, retracing his steps back to the car. Fucking lazy bastards in the council couldn't be bothered coming here to plough the snow.

'What happened to you?' Winston asked as Davidson got back behind the wheel. 'How's yer troosers all wet?'

'I slipped and fell.' Davidson started the car up and put the blue lights on.

'I bet you pished yourself.'

'Fuck off.' He guided the car back out onto the road and floored it. At least this road had been graced by the road gritter's presence and although it was wet with the falling snow, it was driveable.

'I wonder where that arsehole's in such a hurry to get to,' Davidson said. 'He must be blind. Obviously, he doesn't see the snow coming down.'

'It was a hearse,' Winston said.

'What? Away.'

'I'm telling you, it was a hearse. If he doesn't watch what he's doing, he'll be the one in the back of it.'

Davidson took the corner fast and the car shot forward. 'Mental bastard. Who drives a hearse like that in this weather? Did you see the plate or anything?'

'I know I'm good, but I'm not that fucking good. Chucking it down with snow and the radge is giving it the welly, and you think I can read a number plate? It was very inconsiderate of him not to slow down so I could have a wee deek at it.'

'Aye, that's shan. There's nae respect nowadays. He could have pulled over and waited for us, knowing we were going to gie it the welly and catch the bastard anyway.'

Both men laughed.

'I'll call it in,' said Winston.

Davidson sat forward in his seat, looking out the windscreen as the snow blasted towards them almost horizontally. It was like being on the bridge of the *Enterprise* watching stars coming at the window.

Up a hill, keeping the car in a lower gear, the blue lights bouncing off the snow.

'I wonder where the bastard's going at this time of night?' Davidson said.

Winston looked at his watch; almost one-thirty in the morning. Almost time to head back to the station for a cuppa and a piss. Well, a cuppa for Davidson anyway.

'Christ, this is the arse end of town. This just leads out into the wilds. What's he playing at?' Davidson said, more thinking aloud than asking a question.

'Maybe an accident.'

'We would have heard about it on the radio, Stan.'

'That's true. Besides, he's hooring it a bit fast for going to an accident. And wouldn't they send their van rather than the meat wagon?'

'Aye. There's no way one of those old things would be sent out here. He's driving it like he's just stolen it.'

Davidson looked at Winston. Maybe somebody had stolen it.

They crested the brow of a hill and the road was slick up here. Even more slick on the way down on the other side, as Davidson found out.

At the bottom of the hill, the car slid sideways into a snowbank and bounced off, spinning round until they were facing the opposite direction.

Both men looked down the small side road in the

middle of the bend. Where the old, abandoned church was.

Where the hearse was.

Its red taillights were on and steam was coming out of the front end. The driver's door was wide open.

As was the rear tailgate.

Davidson put the car in gear and slowly drove along the narrow road and turned into the churchyard where the hearse was.

He stopped behind it. The coffin that had been in the back was now out of it, propped up at an angle. It had slid partway out and was sitting precariously against the open back end.

'Fuck me,' Davidson said. 'Call it in, Stan.'

Winston got on the radio again as Davidson left the warmth of the car and got out into the falling snow.

The headlights were still working, lighting up the old church. It had fallen into disrepair a long time ago, and if it had been in an inner city, it would have been tagged with graffiti by now.

He started walking towards the hearse, or more specifically, the coffin.

The driver wasn't in the vehicle. Footprints led away round the old building, but Davidson wasn't in the mood for a chase on foot.

'Boo!'

Something grabbed Davidson on either side of his waist and he jumped round.

Winston was standing there grinning at him.

'Ya daft bastard. I nearly took you down with one of my deadly ju-jitsu moves.'

'Nearly shat yourself, more like. And since when do you do ju-jitsu?'

'I would have battered you over the napper with my baton. That's almost like ju-jitsu.'

Winston laughed and nodded to the coffin. 'What the hell is that? I mean, I know what it is, but it's a hearse crashed into an old church with a coffin hanging out of its arse. You couldn't make this up.'

'The lid's not on right,' Davidson said. 'It isn't screwed down. Like your heid.'

They looked at each other, as if thinking, *You go first.*

The gravestones over at the side were covered with snow and the graveyard itself was covered. This made the whole scene lighter than it would have been had there been no snow.

'Open it,' Winston said in a low voice.

'Nobody can hear you,' Davidson said. 'And why don't *you* open it?'

'Because you're bigger than I am. I'll watch your back.'

'Keep your fucking hands to yourself. Or I'll tell them all at the station you touched me in a graveyard.'

'I'll tell them you pished yourself.'

'Bastard. You owe me big time,' Davidson said.

'Aye, aye, whatever. Just open the thing.'

Davidson straightened up. At least this was a story they could tell in the canteen. With a little embellishment, of course, and leaving out the part where he was having a piss in the bushes.

He moved forward gingerly, his boots crunching on the unploughed car park. The small church looked imposing at this ungodly hour. There was no noise except for the whistle of the wind through the trees.

He reached down to grab the coffin lid. They could both see where the bottom had shifted, but they couldn't see inside. He grabbed it with both hands, thinking that if the driver was in here hiding, Davidson would break the lid over the bastard's face.

He jumped back, preparing to swing it. Then he dropped the lid on the snow.

Winston went over to the bushes at the side of the car park and threw up.

Davidson just stared at what was inside. And he stayed that way until backup arrived.

FOURTEEN

'There's my pal!' Jimmy Dunbar said to his iPad screen as his dog, Scooby, came into view.

'I swear he misses you more every time you go away,' Cathy said.

'I know, hen. But it's my own fault. When Harry McNeil took charge of the new MIT, they asked Calvin Stewart who they thought would be a good choice from the Glasgow side, and he put my name forward. Now whenever a team's needed elsewhere, the four of us get sent. That was one of the stipulations on Harry's part, that he was prepared to travel.'

Cathy laughed. 'I'm not having a dig, love. Just pointing out that our daft dug misses his dad whenever he's away.'

'Keeps you warm in bed, though, eh?' Dunbar smiled at her.

'He does that.'

'Better him than the window cleaner.'

'Or the milkman.'

'You've taken that too far.' It was his favourite line from *Chewin' the Fat*. They both laughed.

They chatted idly about their day, Dunbar keeping his end of the story to the bare bones.

'It's freezing up here. But Alex took a bad turn earlier.'

'Oh no. What's wrong?'

'She was sick. To be honest, I think she's pregnant. Or she ate something that didn't agree with her. My money's on the former.'

'Poor lass. Harry will look after her.'

'He will, aye.'

Just then Dunbar's phone rang. It was the Blairgowan station.

'Hold on a minute, love, while I answer this.'

He took the phone call and listened to the caller before hanging up. 'Guess what?'

'You got a shout.'

'I did. I was looking forward to having a wee dram later too. Duty calls.'

'Better get your long johns back on.'

'I didn't have a chance to take them off. Give Scooby a hug from his dad. Love you.'

'Love you too.'

Cathy was sitting with the dog, and Dunbar waved goodbye to them. For a man who took no shite off anybody, he was a sap when it came to his family. Just like Harry McNeil.

He grabbed his coat and locked the door to his room before going along to knock on Harry's door.

'We got a shout, Harry. Somewhere out of town. In an old graveyard.'

He heard Alex retching again.

'Jesus, does she need a doctor?'

'I'm not sure to be honest.' Harry stepped out into the hallway and pulled the door almost closed. 'She's pregnant, Jimmy.'

'Christ, I suspected that, friend. I am a detective.'

'The thing is, Morag was never like this. Puking yes, but not like this. It just makes me worry about her.'

'You can stay with her, pal. I don't want you to leave her alone.'

Suddenly, the door was pulled open. Alex was standing with a towel at her face.

'Give me two minutes and I'll be ready, Jimmy. Just need to get my shoes on.'

Both men looked at each other. Her face was white and her eyes were red.

'And brush my teeth too, of course.'

'I'll be right there, Jimmy,' Harry said, closing the door.

'You sure you're okay to go out?' he asked Alex.

'Look at you, acting all macho. Me caveman, look after cavewoman.' She smiled. 'Yes, I'll be fine.'

They got ready and found Dunbar waiting downstairs in the big Land Rover.

'Bloody thing doesn't heat up until you shove a box of matches into the upholstery.'

Strapped in, they took off from the small car park opposite the hotel. The snow was coming down thick and fast.

'Where's Robbie?' Harry asked.

'He was going to Christmas Land. I asked him to keep an eye on that Martin Blair laddie. See who he's been hanging out with down there. I have a gut feeling about him.' Dunbar looked in his mirror at Alex sitting in the back, huddled inside her jacket. 'Don't worry, I won't have you pissing about with Google Maps. I told Sergeant Lamb to make sure one of his uniforms meets us along the road to guide us. The bastard better be there.'

She was. Dunbar had put the blue flashers on so the uniform could see him, and she was waving a torch about. He stopped for her.

'You'll be DCI Dunbar?' she said after Dunbar rolled the window down.

'Either that or these two strange men are about to ruin your day.'

'Ignore them,' Alex said, opening the back door. 'Come in out of the cold.'

The uniform jumped in and looked between the seats at Dunbar. 'Right at the next intersection. Up the hill and round the corner.'

He did as she instructed. Left, right, round the bend, and they passed the little car park where Davidson and Winston had started off their chase.

Five minutes later, they were easing down the hill where the other vehicles with blue lights were waiting.

'Jesus,' Dunbar said as the big vehicle slipped a bit, but he corrected it.

He stopped at the entrance to the graveyard and saw the hearse lit up by other vehicles and some generator-powered lights.

'Just shout if you need me, sir,' the uniform said, getting out of the car.

'Will do.' The dome lights came on for a second until the young woman closed the door.

'What the hell is this?' Harry said. He was looking at the open coffin.

They got out of the car and walked over. Ewan Gibson was there again, dressed in his forensics suit.

'Again with fucking up the crime scene,' he said by way of welcome.

'Tell us what you have here,' Dunbar said, pulling a hat on.

'I'll give you a fiver if you can guess.' Gibson nodded towards the open coffin and the body inside.

'How about you just tell me and I don't get upset?' Dunbar said.

'Jesus. I bet you're fun at games night.'

'Put it this way, he always wins,' Harry said.

'Anyway, *Sherlock*, the body in the coffin is old. Really old. It's skeletonised, with just some of the skin stuck on the bones. There's dirt inside, stuck to the skull and other bones.'

'It was dug up?' Harry said.

'You can come round to games night, my friend. My wife would love to have you on her team, because unlike the great DCI Dunbar there, I am not a loser. She needs a winner on her team.'

'The coffin doesn't look that old,' Dunbar said, itching to skelp the forensics man but ignoring his dig instead.

'It isn't. In my professional opinion, that woman was dug up and put into this newer coffin and was being taken somewhere.'

Harry looked around and saw some uniforms standing around. He called one of them over.

'Who called this in?'

'Me and Stan, I mean PC Winston, were out on patrol,' Alan Davidson said, 'when we stopped to turn around at the car park along the road. This hearse came booting, I mean speeding, round the corner and we gave chase.'

'Did you see who was driving it?'

'No, sir. It was going too fast. When we caught up with it, it was like this, as you see it. The driver was gone.'

'Assuming he hadn't lost control, where would he have ended up – where does this road lead to?'

'Nowhere. It's just a small road that leads to a hiking trail. It goes round in a loop and there are houses at the top, but that's all. That's why the gritters come round and salt the road. Not very often, like, but they do manage now and again.'

'Thanks. I'll read your full report tomorrow.'

Davidson walked away and Harry looked round for Alex, but she was nowhere to be seen. He started looking for her and saw her standing in the graveyard next to a tall gravestone. He could see the vomit at the side of the marker.

'Christ, Harry, I never thought being pregnant was going to be like this.'

'If I'd known, I would never have had you come up here with me. You need to be in bed.'

'I need to be here. A woman was murdered and we've got to give it a hundred per cent to try to catch whoever did it.'

He walked over to Alex and put a hand on her

shoulder, averting his eyes from the yellow snow. 'You need to go back to the hotel.'

'I'll be fine,' she said.

'You don't get to be a hero, not when you're carrying my baby,' he said, but then Alex was falling into his arms, a dead weight.

'Jimmy! I need help! Over here!' he shouted, and Dunbar ran over, along with the uniforms.

'She passed out. We need to get her to a hospital.'

'Say no more, chief.' Dunbar turned to the uniforms. 'Get this woman into the Land Rover. We need to get her help as soon as.'

Harry helped carry Alex, and once she was in the back with the female officer who had shown them the way, they were off.

Harry couldn't help thinking that Alex looked like she was dead.

FIFTEEN

It was getting late, but Robbie Evans had no intention of going back to the hotel just yet. Muckle was walking about with Sparky and Shug, which left him alone with Vern.

'Martin hasn't left the stall all night,' he said, looking over at Martin Blair, who was busy talking with the owner of the stall.

Vern was stamping her feet. 'He's been there every day. Erica doesn't seem to mind him hanging around. She's one of the regular stall-holders apparently.' She looked at her watch. 'They'll start closing up shortly and then the stalls will shut down for the night. Then we're finished. If you fancy coming into the house for a coffee?'

'That would be great.'

They walked round more of the stalls, but there

were few people left looking at all the goods for sale. Santa's grotto was closed now, its last day Christmas Eve.

'Christmas Land has been going for thirty years,' Vern said. 'I was looking at some of the photos hanging in one of the hallways. The skiers love coming here. I don't see the attraction myself, but it's got bigger over the years.'

'But it only opens in December, doesn't it?' Evans said.

'Technically, the end of November, but its last day is Hogmanay.'

'Where do you go from here?'

'Back home. To Glasgow. I'm an old friend of Shug's and he said they needed a new security member this year, so I joined the team.'

They walked near to Erica's stall. It sold imported, handcrafted goods from Europe. Or tat, as Evans called it.

'Evening, Miss Vern,' Martin said.

'Good evening, Martin,' Vern said, smiling at the young man.

Martin didn't look as if he was having mental health issues. Maybe spending all that time in the psychiatric hospital had helped him get a handle on things. It couldn't be easy finding your friend hanging from a tree.

'Hello, Erica,' Vern said as the young woman popped back up from bending down behind the counter.

'Oh, hello, Vern. How're things going?'

'Same as usual. We're here in case scallies like you start any nonsense.' Vern laughed. 'Erica Sibbald, this is DS Robbie Evans.'

'Pleased to meet you, Robbie Evans.'

'Likewise,' Evans said.

'I have to admit, things have been quite good this year. And I got me a new helper. I'll be sad to see this place close down again. It's my favourite spot.'

'Do you travel around?' Evans asked.

'Oh, no. I own a shop in town, selling skiing gear. You wouldn't believe the numpties who come up here and they've forgotten to pack something. Or they break something, lose something. You name it, I have that something in my shop. But I do this for fun. My manager runs the shop for me. It's like having a break, coming here.'

'I like helping out too. Miss Sibbald says I can help out in her shop later, when I get some training.'

'That's terrific, Martin,' Vern said.

Evans's phone rang. He answered it.

'Hello?'

'It's Dunbar, Robbie. We're over at the hospital.

Alex collapsed. I just wanted you to know where we're at, in case you need to get hold of us.'

'I'll be right over.' He hung up and turned to Vern and explained what had happened.

'Give her my best,' Vern said and watched as Evans walked away.

Martin was looking at her.

And he wasn't smiling anymore.

SIXTEEN

'You've nothing to worry about,' doctor Carter said, smiling down at Alex. He turned to Harry, who was standing anxiously behind him. 'It's extreme morning sickness. Called hyperemesis gravidarum. It happens to some mothers-to-be. We just need to give her some medicine and that will take care of things. Plus she'll be on the IV, because she was starting to get dehydrated. It's nothing to worry about. Some women get it when they're pregnant.'

'Thanks, Doctor,' Harry said.

'However,' Carter said to Alex, 'you'll need some bed rest. At least a few days. Then you'll be up and about again. But I'd rather keep you in, just to keep an eye on things.' He smiled at her.

'Thank you.' Her voice was weak and she felt tired.

'I'll leave you both alone now. If you need anything, just press the button and a nurse will come.'

Carter left the room and Harry sat down on the bed next to her.

'Knock, knock,' Dunbar said, opening the door a fraction. 'Everybody decent?'

'Come in, Jimmy,' Harry said. 'Did you expect me to be running about in my skids or something?'

'You never know with you. Look at you; the poor lassie's knackered and you're trying to worm your way under the covers.'

Harry laughed.

'Come in, Jimmy,' Alex said as Dunbar closed the door. 'Thank you for putting up with me.'

'Och, don't be daft. Shit happens to all of us.'

Just then there was a rapid knocking at the door. Dunbar stood up and opened it. Evans was standing there, out of breath.

'Get in here. Did you run all the way?'

'Just up the stairs.'

'Look at the state of him. Too many bloody bacon rolls. You need to eat more yoghurt, son.'

But Evans walked past Dunbar and stood at the end of the bed. 'Is everything okay?'

'She's fine, pal,' Harry said. 'Extreme sickness.'

'Thank God. I drove here as fast as I could. Muckle

wanted to come over, but they wouldn't have let Sparky in, so I promised I'd let him know.'

'Good man.'

'Thanks for coming in, Robbie,' said Alex, 'but I'll be up and about in a couple of days. I feel like a fool.'

'She passed out in the graveyard and we got her here,' said Harry. 'Luckily, there were plenty of bodies on hand. If you see what I mean.'

'It's nice you're concerned for me, but it's just sickness. I'll be right as rain. I don't want to let the team down.'

'What?' Dunbar said. 'Away with yourself. You're not letting anybody down. Besides, we have Muckle and the others to give us backup if we need it. I wouldn't put too much hope in the uniforms around here.'

'Good,' Evans said. 'Call me if you need anything.'

'Thanks, Robbie.'

'Right, laddie, let's give this couple some peace,' said Dunbar. 'Although I think this one here has already done the damage.'

'He's an animal right enough,' Alex said.

'You're just encouraging him,' Harry said.

'Catch you later this morning.' Dunbar and Evans left Harry alone with his wife.

'Christ, you scared me,' Harry said.

'I scared myself. One minute I was throwing up

against some poor person's headstone, the next I was in here.'

'I don't think the dead person will mind.'

'Not the point. Anyway, what's the latest on the body in the coffin?'

'It's old.'

'I don't understand what it was doing in a hearse.'

'Nobody does. Yet. We're having a meeting first thing in the morning.' He looked at the clock on the wall. 'Later this morning.'

She put a hand on his. 'Go get some rest. I can't afford to have you knackered as well.'

'I will. I'm feeling it now. I'll be drinking coffee like it's going out of fashion tomorrow.' He looked at her for a moment, questions rolling around inside his head. 'Are you going to tell your parents you're pregnant?'

'No. They washed their hands of me.'

'It's their grandchild. It might be a way of building bridges.'

Alex looked away from him for a moment. 'I'll think about it, okay? Just give me some time.'

'Okay. I won't pressure you. I just wanted you to know that I'll stick by whatever you decide.'

'Thank you.'

Harry leaned down and gave her a kiss. 'Promise me you won't come back to work until you feel fit?'

'I promise.'

He stopped at the door and smiled at her, and then walked along the quiet hallway. One half of him wanted nothing more to do with Alex's parents after the way they had treated her, but he was willing to start with a clean slate.

SEVENTEEN

The two men sat in the dark room, only the light from the log fire illuminating their faces.

'He crashed the hearse,' the first one said matter-of-factly. 'That was deliberate.'

'Jesus. He's drawing attention to the body. He wanted to get the police to look into it. We're screwed.'

'Maybe we should just go to the police and tell them everything.'

'That wouldn't get us anywhere, except prison,' the second man said. 'I have no intention of going into a big house where spin the bottle means not being able to sit for a week.'

'Why now? Why is he doing this?' The first man got up out of his chair and went to the window. It was snowing outside, which used to look good, but now it was just a pain. He turned back to the other man. 'If they catch him, then it will all come crashing down anyway.'

'I'd rather take the risk.' The second man looked at his friend. 'He's hiding in plain sight. He'll leave and go to new hunting ground. Now, go and pour us a drink.'

EIGHTEEN

Jimmy Dunbar and Robbie Evans were eating breakfast when Harry came down.

'Did you call the hospital?' Dunbar said.

'I did. She's fine. They'll keep an eye on her today,
then they'll release her this afternoon.'

'Take whatever time you need, friend. The young
toerag here and I have got things in hand.' Dunbar bit
into a slice of toast and washed it down with some
coffee as Harry grabbed something to eat.

'I want to go and talk to Shug's husband, David,'
said Dunbar. 'He writes real-life crime books. He's
interested in this case, since it's happening while he's
here. I thought maybe you could go to the mortuary –'

'Listen, Jimmy,' Harry cut in, 'there's something
you should know about me. I hate the bloody mortuary.
Yes, yes, I've been hundreds of times, but it gets my

guts rolling every single time. It's the smell of the place.'

'Okay, Robbie and I will go along. We'll keep you in the loop.'

'If that was me,' said Evans, 'you'd call me a fanny.'

'You are a fanny. Harry's earned his keep on the force, son. When you've got the same service as he has, you can delegate who goes to the mortuary. Meantime, get your breakfast finished so we can go and find out about that skeleton. And find out when the hearse was nicked.' Dunbar turned to Harry. 'The old boy at the funeral director's place didn't even know somebody had choried his hearse.'

'Does he have cameras?'

'We'll find out later.' Dunbar held up his cup, waving it about in front of Evans.

'What?' Evans said.

'I think I can hear a plane coming over.'

Evans shook his head. 'Give me your cup then.'

Dunbar grinned as Evans went to top up the coffees.

'He was shagging Linda Fry, wasn't he?' Harry said in a low voice. 'And now you're blackmailing him.'

'My lips are sealed,' Dunbar said, smiling.

'Are you going to put him out of his misery?'

'Let me have some fun first.'

NINETEEN

Harry had asked for a pool car from the station and a uniform brought him a Vauxhall. He drove over to the hospital. When he stepped out of the lift, he saw Alex's doctor standing talking to Dudley Matthews, the therapist.

Harry walked along to Alex's room and found her sitting up in bed.

'Morning, honey,' he said to her. 'How are you feeling?'

'Better. But I can't even look at food. Jesus, just the thought –'

'Don't talk about it. Focus on something else. Like me?' He beamed a smile at her.

'Come over here and give your wife a kiss, dafty.'

He kissed her gently, not wanting to put any weight on her.

'I'm not made of porcelain.' She smiled and Harry didn't want to say that the colour of her skin was like porcelain.

'I saw the doc outside talking to Dudley Matthews,' he said.

'Have you managed to speak with Martin Blair yet?'

'Jimmy and Robbie talked with his grandfather and mother last night. I think they're shielding him. Apparently, he has the mental age of a ten year old, so nobody's looking at him to be the killer. He has alibis, according to his mother, but we need to tread lightly. This could be a PR nightmare if we go in heavy-handed and the press get wind of it.'

'Nobody's saying to go in heavy-handed, but we have to make sure he didn't kill anybody. He's a ten year old trapped in the body of a thirty year old, a man who looks like he could wrestle a bus to the ground.'

'We really can't talk to him without his mother being there. He was cleared the last time when he found his friend. A lot of people think he was guilty because he was a twenty-four-year-old man who had a friend who was only fifteen.'

'It's hard. He could be innocent enough. But if he's been staying at Christmas Land, then people will have seen him. My instinct says it wasn't him, but I've been known to be wrong before.'

'You said it.'

'Cheeky. But seriously, there's no point in chasing our tails.'

'I understand. We have to work out why Martin was released from the hospital and then, soon after, the one girl who almost got caught by the killer was murdered.'

There was a knock on the door and the doctor who was treating Alex stepped into the room.

'How are you feeling, Mrs McNeil?'

'Still a little queasy. But much better than I felt yesterday.'

'Good. It will take a little while for the medicine to kick, maybe a day or so – everybody's different. Make sure you drink plenty of water; stay hydrated. Later this morning, I think we can let you go, but first I want you to have an ultrasound, just to make sure everything is okay. If nothing's amiss, I'll release you. As long as you promise to spend the next couple of days in bed, resting. We want you getting better for Hogmanay, don't we?'

'I will. I promise.'

'Good. I'll have a nurse come in later on and give you a prescription. You can have it filled in the chemist's in town.'

'Thanks, Doctor,' Harry said.

The doctor left the room and Harry brought Alex up to speed on the investigation.

'You going to talk to the funeral director?' she asked him.

'Yes. Jimmy's going to the mortuary, then we're going to talk to Shug's husband, David.'

'I hope this damn sickness goes away soon.'

'It will,' Harry said. 'If you do as you're told.'

'Okay, I'm feeling tired still. And you're annoying me with your lectures. Go and get some bad guys.'

He laughed and kissed her again. 'See you later.'

'Not if I see you first,' she said.

TWENTY

Dunbar and Evans parked the car where Harry and Alex had parked, way in the back of the hospital where the mortuary bay doors were.

'I don't think I could live in a wee town like this,' Evans said.

'What's wrong with it? No lap dance bars or dodgy wee brothels for you to frequent?'

'I don't go to lap dance bars. My new look did all the talking for me. I had no trouble getting a woman.'

They got out of the car into the cold. The snow had stopped for the time being and the sun had made an appearance, but it did bugger all for the temperature. Dunbar had put sunglasses on, but Evans had forgotten his and was shielding his eyes.

'All your new look said was, my bun makes me look like a lassie.'

'Pish. Women love that look.'

'What, the My Little Pony look?'

'Should I be worried that you know about a bairn's toy like that?'

'My granddaughter plays with those things. And stop changing the subject. You looked like a bawbag who could only pull a sixty-year-old granny.'

'She wasn't sixty. You made a mistake there.'

'Really now? You want me to call the station and have somebody ask around, just to be sure?'

'Barely sixty. We had a nice meal out on her birthday. Her idea, not mine.'

'You said you thought she was forty. Lying bastard.' Dunbar pressed the button for the buzzer. 'That must have looked barry in the restaurant. *See that nice young man taking his old maw out for a meal.* Tell me you at least had the decency to pull a beamer.'

'Christ, you make it sound pervy now.'

'It is fucking pervy.'

'What's pervy?' a female voice said. A young woman was standing with the door open.

'Nothing for you to poke your neb into there, hen,' Dunbar said. They showed their warrant cards.

'Mortuary assistant Stacey Nichols. I met your polis pals last night. You're more exciting, though. Tell me what's pervy. We need some excitement up here.'

'Dead skiers not exciting enough for you?' Dunbar

said as they stepped inside and Stacey shut the door behind them. He took his sunglasses off.

'Ah, that's old hat by now. I need something to spice up my life.'

'If you don't keep that nose ring clean, I'm sure sepsis will give you a run for your money. Your boss in?'

'I'm so clean, I squeak when I walk,' she said, walking along a corridor.

'That's something you have in common with my boss here. He's so tight, he squeaks when he walks,' Evans said.

'You've taken that too far,' Dunbar said.

Stacey laughed. 'Never mind, DS Evans, my boss is tight as well.'

'I can detect a lack of respect for people who are not only your elders but also your bosses,' Dunbar said.

She took them to the post-mortem suite, where Dr Valerie Henderson was waiting for them.

'Welcome, gentlemen,' she said, smiling. 'I had a PM this morning, but after your call, I postponed it.'

'Sorry to ruin your schedule,' Dunbar said, not meaning it.

'No, don't worry. This is fascinating.'

They all looked at the skeletal remains that had been inside the coffin, now lying on a steel table.

'Forensics have taken the coffin away for processing. But they found this tucked into it. I photographed it before they took it away, as I knew you would want to see it.'

She picked up a remote and the TV on one wall kicked into life. 'By the wonders of modern technology, I can show you this photo of an old newspaper clipping.'

Everybody stood and looked at the small clipping, which had been blown up to fill the large-screen TV.

Woman Goes Missing at Skiing Resort in the Highlands.

Dunbar read the story. Caitlin McGhee, eighteen, was partying with a group of friends and nobody noticed she was missing until the following day. Despite a wide search, nothing was found. Police carried on searching for her.

There was another photo of people searching in a field, with a dog handler in front. Dunbar noticed the old police uniform, just like he had worn. *A proper uniform,* he thought.

'This was in the coffin, you say?' Dunbar said to Valerie.

'Yes. It was there with the body. The forensics man said he thought it had been put there after the skeleton was put in the coffin, so somebody would find it. It would have decomposed in the ground.'

'Somebody sending us a message?' Dunbar thought

out loud. 'Like they want us to know who this person is. For some reason, they don't want us to waste time trying to solve the mystery of who she is, but would rather tell us outright.'

'It would seem that way.'

'Does this look like somebody who's been in the ground for thirty years?' Evans asked.

'Pretty much,' said Valerie. 'Only the skeleton remains, as you can see, with little bits of skin. Not much else. From what I can see, it looks like she was buried in the ground without having been put in a coffin. When she was in the coffin in the back of the hearse, her body had been wrapped in a new sheet, but previous to that she had been wrapped in some sort of cloth, which in turn was wrapped in heavy plastic. Most of the plastic was intact, holding her in place.'

'Whoever was driving the hearse knew where this young woman was buried and dug her up.'

'Maybe the same person who killed her thirty years ago,' Stacey said. 'Assuming that she was killed, I mean.'

'You have a point,' Evans said.

Dunbar had one last look at the skeleton before looking at the pathologist. 'Thanks, Doc. If you could send over a report of your findings to the station when you're finished.'

TWENTY-ONE

'Right then, young lady, let's be having you,' the porter said, coming into the room with the wheelchair. 'Doc's ordered an ultrasound for you.'

'Yes.' Alex used her maiden name, Maxwell, for professional situations. This was a personal matter, so she was using her married name.

'Hop aboard, and we'll get you down to the magic land where all the fun stuff happens.'

He helped her out of bed and got her into the wheelchair, covering her with a blanket.

'Scream if you want to go faster,' he said, turning around and guiding the chair out of the room with practised ease.

'A nice, slow drive in the country will be fine,' she said as they went to the lift.

Downstairs, on the lower level, there were signs for the radiology department.

'My, my, no skiers today. Usually, there's one of them with a broken leg,' the porter said.

'Don't jinx it.'

'From your lips to God's ears.' He walked round to stand in front of Alex. 'You'll be going through that door there. They'll come out and get you. Shouldn't be long.'

'Thank you.'

He walked away out of sight and she could hear the ding of the lift bell. Then the lift doors slid closed and she was alone. With her thoughts.

She had dreamed of being a mother for a long time, and now she was pregnant, she was filled with joy and excitement. But the sickness hadn't come into play in her vision of pregnancy at all. Yes, the normal morning sickness, but not this debilitating illness. Still, it was going to be worth it. Having Harry's baby. A dream come true.

She smiled when she thought about him –

The wheelchair suddenly started moving quickly as somebody grabbed hold of it from behind and began running.

'What the hell?' she said, trying to put her feet down to stop the chair, but she had hospital socks on and they did nothing to act as brakes.

Then a wall was coming up fast and she crashed into it, the momentum throwing her forward, out of the chair, until her face met the wall. She bounced back and felt her hair being grabbed.

Then something stung her neck.

Then nothing.

TWENTY-TWO

'Aye, as if business isn't bad enough, some bastard comes along and takes one o' me fucking motors.' Tom Birrell, owner of Birrell & Son Funeral Directors, was standing in the middle of the yard with Harry by his side. He was an older man, and Harry thought he looked like he had one foot in the grave.

'This is where it was?' Harry said, nodding to the empty space with the small snow banks forming a rectangle where a vehicle had been sitting. The snow that was coming down was doing its best to fill in the blanks.

'What a great detective you are.' The old man shook his head.

A younger man walked over from the direction of the garage. He was smiling but still looked austere in his black suit with white shirt and black tie.

'Dad, the detective here is only trying to help. They found one of our hearses and he has to know why it was taken.' He smiled at Harry. 'Anderson Birrell. I'm the son in Birrell *and Son* Funeral Directors. Call me Andy.'

Harry felt funny about shaking the hand of a man who dealt in death, so he didn't offer, keeping both hands in his coat pockets.

'I thought business was good round here? Dead skiers, dead car accident victims. I thought you had it made?'

'You thought wrong,' said Birrell Senior. 'A big conglomerate moved into the town up the road, giving me competition. Time was, we independents wouldn't step on each other's toes. We had an unwritten boundary. We would call each other up. *We've got a busload of orphans that are on your side. Need a hand?'*

Busload of orphans? Harry thought. *Jesus.* 'I get the picture. Now you've got a missing hearse that was found with a body in it. It's smashed up, probably beyond repair, and even if it wasn't, it would still be impounded.'

'Christ, if I wanted to hear doom and gloom, I would have put the news on. Talk about the bearer of bad news.'

'Tell me when you noticed it was missing.'

The old man huffed and puffed, and Harry

thought for a moment that he was trying to blow the garage down.

'When you lot called. I live in a flat above the funeral parlour down on the High Street. The vehicles are parked here. Two in the garage, but they're the newer ones. This one was an older model. A bit like my wife; still worked but needed a wee tickle to get going nowadays.'

Harry did his best not to screw his face up. The man had to be seventy if he was a day and God knows what his wife looked like. He tried not to imagine her being tickled, but sometimes the mind ran the film anyway and you were stuck with it.

'I only heard about it this morning from Dad,' said Anderson. 'I live in the flat too, but I was out playing poker with some friends.'

'Poker,' Old Man Birrell said. 'He plays shite. I'm surprised he hasn't lost the fucking business by now.'

'We only play for fun, Dad. If I was going to bet with anything, it would be you. Can you imagine the advert now? Why live in your own place when you can share the same flat as a grumpy old bawbag?'

'Enough of your bloody cheek. You would do well to get your own place instead of carousing with those slappers and getting blootered at the weekends.'

'That was in my younger days. I've grown up now.'

'Bollocks.'

'Is the yard locked?' Harry asked.

'Naw, is it fuck. Who in their right mind would want to chorie a fucking hearse?'

'Dad, for God's sake.'

'Somebody did.' *In his right mind.* There was only one person Harry knew of in town who fit the description of not being in his right mind.

'The coffin in the hearse was new, so we're thinking he might have stolen that too. Was there a coffin in the hearse?'

The old man curled his lip. Made a few sounds as if struggling to find the right expletive. 'No.' He settled on the one-word answer and spat it out like a child might spit out a piece of broccoli.

'We only keep them in the workshop at the back of the garage,' Anderson said.

'Do you know if any are missing?' Harry asked, digging deep for his patience.

'Again, I only got woken up by some of you lot,' said Birrell. 'I mean, I get up early but not that early.'

'Where do you keep your inventory?'

The old man nodded to the garage again. 'In there. It's bigger than it looks from the front. There's a workshop in the back. We make them and store them there.'

'Can we have a look?'

'I suppose so.' Birrell turned from the spot where the car was and walked up to the personnel entrance next to the garage door. It was more like a small ware-house than a garage. He took a key out of his pocket and suddenly stepped back.

'Aw, would you look at that? Some bastard smashed the lock!' He was about to touch it when Harry stopped him.

'Where?' Anderson said. 'Oh, dear. What is this place coming to?'

'I'll take it and put it in a bag. It might have prints on it,' Harry said.

With the lock safely in his pocket, Harry pulled the door open and stepped inside.

'Light switch is on the left,' the old man said, happy now to be behind the detective should somebody come barrelling at them with a shovel.

There was no barrelling, no shovels, only two cars: a hearse and a limo.

'The workshop is through the back,' Anderson said.

They walked past the gleaming black cars, past a little office and through a door into the back. There were two shelves holding coffins and the lower one had an empty space.

'It's gone,' said the old man. He looked at Harry. 'Was the coffin you found dark brown?'

Harry couldn't remember. 'I think so.' Weren't they all the same?

'You think so?'

Anderson stepped in. 'What he means, Chief Inspector, is no, they're all different. To the untrained eye, they might look similar, but they're different.'

Clearly, judging by Birrell's look of incredulity, not all coffins were made the same. 'Hold on.'

Harry took his phone out and looked at the photo he'd taken of the corpse in the coffin, hanging out the back of the hearse.

'Is that it?'

'Jesus. What did the bastard do?' Birrell looked at Harry. 'Yes, that looks like the same one. Expensive bastard it was too.'

'Do you have security cameras?'

'I wish I had now. Any idea who stole it?'

'Not yet. But I don't think it was joyriders.'

TWENTY-THREE

Harry pulled in behind the big police Land Rover and climbed into the back of the behemoth. It wasn't the size of a double-decker, but it felt like it after the Vauxhall.

Dunbar was tossing a coin in the air. He slapped it onto the back of his hand.

'I'm not playing your stupid game,' Evans said.

'What's happening, boys?' Harry asked.

'We're tossing a coin to see who's picking up the tab in the bar tonight,' Dunbar said. 'Call in the air.'

Evans shook his head and sighed. Dunbar tossed the coin.

'Tails,' Evans said.

The coin landed. Dunbar looked at it, saw it was tails and turned his fist into his right palm so it was now heads.

'Loser. Beer's on Robbie.'

'Best of three.'

'Wee bastard.' Dunbar tossed the coin again.

'Heads.'

Dunbar saw it was heads and turned the coin into his palm again. 'Sorry, son.'

'You're cheating.'

'How am I cheating?'

'You just are. I can tell.'

'You can tell heehaw.'

'I can. You always cheat. You're no' right in the heid. It's an illness with you.'

'You hear that, Harry? That's the sound of a sore loser.'

'Call it what you want, I'm still not picking up your drinks tab. You'll just get blootered since you're not paying for it.'

'That's fine, son. We can have a few swallies and then maybe go to the chippie afterwards. There's a nice lassie works in that one in the High Street. What's her name again?'

Evans shook his head. 'Maybe I'll buy a couple.'

'He always comes round to my way of thinking,' Dunbar said, smiling. Then to Harry: 'How did you get on with that crabbit old bastard?'

'How do you know he's crabbit?'

'Because when you left, he called the station

complaining about you. Said you didn't have a clue who stole his hearse. He was in a right strop, the sergeant said.'

'He was not a happy camper. But the hearse and coffin came from that funeral director's place right enough,' Harry told Dunbar and Evans. 'His son, Anderson Birrell, was nicer. I think the old boy needs to retire. He saw nothing because he lives above the parlour in the High Street and the garage and work-shop are in the wilds. How did you get on?'

'A newspaper clipping was put in the coffin along with the body,' Dunbar said. 'Somebody wants us to know who she was.'

'Somebody dug her up, then gave us her name. Was the clipping a photocopy or an original?'

'Original,' Evans said.

'Right,' said Harry, 'let's get on inside Shug and David's place and we'll see what the computer whizz has for us.'

The bungalow was in a nice part of town, in a street with other decent houses. They trudged through the snow, glad to see somebody had been out shovelling.

Shug answered the door. 'Come away in. The kettle's on.'

They cleared their boots as best they could before

going through to the living room. A gas fire was working in tandem with the central heating.

'David likes it a bit cooler, but I can't sleep in a cold house,' said Shug. 'He even has a fan on in the winter. I think he was conceived in an igloo.'

David was on his computer in a small dining room off the living room, next to the open-plan kitchen.

'Shug and I are at opposite ends of the scale when it comes to hot and cold,' he said.

'Go on, tell him, it's best to be warm in the winter,' Shug said.

Sensing a domestic might break out, Harry walked over to David. Then he turned to Shug. 'You said the kettle was on? I like my coffee with just a small dash of milk.'

'Nae bother. You two?'

'Same,' Dunbar said. He'd been to some houses where he would rather drink the toilet water, but this was a decent place with friends.

'Well, make yourselves comfortable.'

They sat down on chairs and the settee where they could see David.

'We were hoping you could help us out with some history of the murders,' Dunbar said. 'If you have all the background collated.'

'I was putting everything together this morning,' said David. 'I was up late doing some research and found out some stuff that may be on the border between fascinating and total crap.'

'Let's hear it, son, and we'll decide. Give us what you've got.'

Shug came in with the coffees and they listened to what David had to say.

'I got all this stuff from news archives. Thirty years ago, the Christmas Land market opened up and it was a hit with all the skiers and visitors to the area. It's gradually expanded over the years. Started by the Blair family.' David turned to look at them. 'Did you know the town was started back in the early nineteen hundreds by two men, Blair and Gowan?'

'We do now,' Dunbar said. 'Were they a couple of psychopathic killers?'

'Alas, Jimmy, I don't have the answer to that. However, I was reading about Caitlin McGhee, the eighteen year old who went missing thirty years ago. She was a local. But she wasn't the only one who went missing. Two young women went missing at the same time.

'The two women were last seen together, going to a Christmas party. Susan was nineteen at the time. Anna, eighteen. They were supposedly meeting a group of friends, and later on, when questioned, all the friends said they never turned up. The police searched for them, but no trace of them was ever found. Their bank accounts were never used and they left behind their belongings. And now we know that Caitlin was murdered. Or at least buried. We have to assume the fate of the other two was exactly the same.'

David turned from his computer and drank some of the coffee his husband had made.

'Can you check and see how many women have gone missing from around here over the years?' asked Dunbar.

'I already did. I was doing research to see whether a true crime book would be viable and I came across something interesting. No more women went missing, but plenty have died in the region. And I don't mean from natural causes as such. There have been horrendous accidents.'

'This place seems to be the accident capital of Europe, by all accounts,' Harry said.

'Plenty of people die on the ski slopes, and the amount of car crashes is ridiculous. Britain doesn't want to spend money on motorways or even dual carriageways. If you look at a map, you'll see there isn't a direct motorway link from the capital of Scotland to the capital of England. The government doesn't want to spend the money to upgrade the roads...but don't get me started on that.'

David drank more coffee and Dunbar hoped it was decaf.

'Okay, so plenty of people have died in the region over the years. But I started making a table of young women who died aged between fifteen and twenty-five. There have been twelve. In groups of three. I mean, it's not definitive, but it stood out.'

'How did they die?' Evans asked.

David turned back to his computer. 'Let's take a group at random. Twelve years ago, a girl was found impaled on a branch on a hiking trail. Another girl drowned in the river, just outside of town. A third was found with her neck broken, her head lying against a rock at the bottom of a hill. All three of them had a high blood-alcohol level in their system. All of them worked at Christmas Land.'

'What did the pathologist at the time rule the deaths?' Dunbar asked.

'Accidental. I looked at their death certificates online. I had to pay for them, of course, because Scotland charges to look at records, but it was worth it.'

'And there're more like that?' Harry said.

'Oh, yes,' said David. 'A girl found at the side of the road, dead. It was ruled accidental after they figured she'd been involved in a hit-and-run.'

'Alcohol in her system?' Dunbar said. 'Worked at Christmas Land?'

'Yes and yes.'

Harry sat up. 'Now we have two girls who were

murdered six years ago and one who got away when someone tried to abduct her – and now she's dead too. Why has he changed from making it look like an accident to outright killing them?'

'The only different factor I can see here is Martin Blair. I think he's the key,' Dunbar said.

'Plus girls have been listed as missing over the years,' said David. 'Not all at the same time, of course. And since there are so many foreign visitors to the area, who's to say he didn't take foreigners from here?'

'Can you bring up a map of this area?' Harry said.

'Absolutely.' David googled a map of Scotland and zoomed in when it came up.

'Can you find the Blairgowan estate on there?'

He moved his fingers on the trackpad and then they were looking at a satellite view of the town of Blairgowan.

'The estate is right there,' David said, tapping the screen with a pen. But it had a little symbol that Google had put on the image, indicating the where the estate was.

Harry looked at the image. 'I just want to see where the big house is in relation to where Carol was found hanged. And what's beyond it.'

He pointed his finger at the screen without actually touching it. He saw the house, the back lawn behind it. The pathway went into the woods and he lost the exact spot. But there was a hiking trail that came out on the other side. Across the hill would be the car park. When they had found blood on the trail where Carol was hanged, the uniformed sergeant had said footprints went over the hill towards the car park. The same car park where the uniforms were last night, where they started chasing the hearse from.

He traced the road with his finger in the air. There were more hiking trails that ran near a small loch. The road went up and around, and there were houses and he saw the funeral director's garage.

'He stole the hearse and coffin from this point here,' Harry said, pointing with his finger. 'He crashed down here, at the site of the old church. Somewhere in between these two points, he dug up Caitlin's corpse.' He turned to Dunbar. 'We don't know where. It isn't obvious.'

Dunbar stood up. 'Show me where the garage is on the map.'

David scooted his chair back to let the detectives have a closer look.

'There's the garage,' Harry said, pointing again.

'He went there and choried the hearse, then for some reason came booting down...from where?' said Dunbar.

'We'll ask around, see if anybody has any ideas.'

Harry turned to David. 'Thanks for your help,

David. I hope you can get this new book off the ground.'

'I already have, Harry.'

'I think we should go and talk to the Blair family again,' Dunbar said. 'I want to know why somebody chose their property to hang young girls on.'

'Meet you over there,' said Harry.

They left the house and drove off under a broken sky that was spilling snow down onto them.

TWENTY-FOUR

Muckle McInsh was getting ready to go downstairs with Sparky to let him burn off some steam when he happened to look out of his window onto the back lawn.

His room was small, although there were plenty of empty rooms that were bigger than his. He supposed this was where the staff had stayed back in the day, and he couldn't complain because he was getting it rent-free and they let the dog stay with him. He wouldn't have taken the job if he couldn't bring Sparky. Besides, the dog was earning his keep, patrolling the shitey market stalls.

Something caught his eye. Movement, on the edge of the property, near the trail that led into the woods.

He took out a pair of binoculars – the perv glasses, Shug called them – and focused them on the woods.

A man with a beard was standing there.

The killer returning to the scene?

He picked up his phone and called Vern. 'Where are you?' he asked her.

'*Down in the kitchen. Why?*'

'Beardy's creeping about near the path on the other side of the lawn.'

'*What? Our killer?*'

'Could be. I'm coming down with the boy. Just getting his jacket on.'

'*I'm going to check it out.*'

'Not without me, Vern! Stay there!'

But she had hung up.

'Fuck.'

Sparky sensed something was going down and for once he didn't make an arse of himself but stood still while his K9 jacket was put on.

Then he went berserk.

TWENTY-FIVE

Vern looked out one of the many kitchen windows and just saw the back of the black coat disappearing from view into the woods.

Technically, being private security, they weren't allowed to carry weapons, but it was alright for politicians to say that from the comfort of Holyrood while they had police protection outside.

Vern had an extendable baton acquired through a friend, handcuffs and gloves that had weighted knuckle joints. Plus she knew how to fight.

She ran across the snow on the back lawn. There was no way to conceal her movements, so the next best option was speed.

Her breathing was faster as she entered the woods, jogging up the hiking trail. If he saw her, then too bad. She couldn't conceal the fact that she was security, but she tried to stay as close to the tree line as possible.

She reached the point where the young girl had been hanged and stopped, looking around her. The trees were thicker here, blocking out a lot of the light. She stood and listened, but there was only the sound of the wind blowing the snow.

She was about to walk forward when she heard a foot crunching snow behind her.

He was good, she would give him that.

He had got to within six feet of her before she heard him. He was good. Just not as good as she was.

She turned round fast. He had reached a hand out to grab her. She grabbed it, twisted it and kicked his leg out from beneath him.

He yelled and fell on his back.

'Fackin' 'ell. Let me go!' The accent was pure East London.

Vern stood up when she heard her two boys coming.

The man with the beard rolled onto his back and was greeted by the sight of a snarling German shepherd inches from his face.

'You fucking move and you'll wish you'd been the one who was hanged!' Muckle shouted at him.

'Roll on your front,' Vern instructed him, bringing out her handcuffs.

'This is not what it looks like,' the man said, but he rolled over anyway.

TWENTY-SIX

'He is who he says he is,' Harry said, throwing the man's driving licence down on the kitchen table.

'Means fuck all,' Dunbar said.

Gary Whitman sat with a mug of coffee, still shaking from being barked at by Sparky, who was sitting close by, next to Muckle, itching to have a real go at the man who had been shouting at his dad.

'Listen, I know what this all looks like. It ain't anything like it. I used to be one of you lot until I retired.' Whitman looked at Vern. 'Yeah, you 'eard right, *retired*. I don't do much fightin' these days. Bit long in the tooth for that.'

'You were spotted at a murder scene where a young lassie was hanged. I don't know what you do about that down where you come from, but we're no' quite as lenient as you, pal.' Dunbar leaned on the chair, and

Evans was standing off to the side, like he was about to get free and fancy with some clever footwork should the older man start to cause a rumpus.

'Let me explain, alright? Before you dish out some vigilante justice. And if we can all sit down, this will go a lot easier.'

'You try and run for it, pal, and my dug will have chewed you a new arsehole before you get close to the door.'

Whitman held up his hands. 'I've got a bad back, son. I ain't runnin' nowhere, trust me.'

They sat down round the table, Dunbar, Evans, Vern and Harry. Whitman reached into an inside pocket.

'You keep your fucking hands where we can see them,' Dunbar said, and Sparky stood up, growling.

'I was searched for weapons and I don't have any. What I do have is my old warrant card.' Whitman brought it out and showed it to Dunbar.

Dunbar looked at it: DCI Gary Whitman, with the word 'retired' stamped over it. He handed it back.

'Not your usual neck of the woods, is it?' Harry asked.

'No, it's not. I'm here because I knew there was going to be another death. And I was right.'

'How did you know that?' Dunbar said. 'Because you're a killer?'

'No. I knew it was going to happen because I've been tracking the killer for the past ten years. I retired two months ago, but I knew that bastard was still out there. I've never been able to track him. He's very clever, this guy.'

'What guy?' Dunbar asked.

Whitman looked at them before answering. 'He doesn't have an official name. But I call him *Infinity*. And he's been killing for thirty years.'

'How can he have been killing for thirty years and got away with it for so long without getting caught?' Evans said.

'He's very clever,' Whitman said again. 'Now, I don't have any definitive proof that he's been killing for thirty years, but it's a theory I've been working on for years.'

Harry picked up the warrant card and walked away with it to call David again.

'What made you first think this?' Dunbar said.

'It was thirty years ago. A friend of my guv'nor's came in and I heard them talking. His daughter had been up here with friends on a skiing holiday and she'd disappeared. He was going off his head. He called your lot up here and they did a search. She was found dead, a needle in her arm. She'd never done drugs in her life, her father said. And guess where she was found.'

They all looked blankly at him.

'No takers? In the cemetery where the hearse crashed.'

'They wrote it off as an accidental overdose?' Evans said.

'They did indeed, my friend. This bloke, the friend of me boss, he swore blind she wouldn't do that sort of thing. Turns out, her and her friends were smoking weed, but they all said she wouldn't take the hard stuff.'

'It's hardly conclusive, pal,' Dunbar said.

'Wait. I haven't finished. They were packing up, getting ready to come home, when one of the other girls went off on her own. They found her hanging in the cemetery where the first girl was found. They said she blamed herself for supplying the drugs. There was a note found. Scrawled, written like she was drunk. It was ruled a suicide.'

'You don't think it was?' Harry said.

'I wouldn't have thought otherwise, but this friend of me boss was adamant. He was convinced. Me boss asked me to look into it. When I did, I discovered that after the hanging, a young girl was found dead inside the church. She'd been drinking. There was an empty bottle of whisky by her side. She'd choked on her own vomit. The thing was, there was a tablet found nearby. A sleeping tablet. There were none in her system, and it was shrugged off. They didn't connect it to the girl.'

'Maybe that was his Plan B,' Dunbar said. 'He

could have forced her to drink, trying to make her vomit. He could have put a hand over her nose and mouth. If she didn't vomit, he'd have forced the pills down her throat.'

Whitman pointed a finger at him. 'I would have liked you on my team, my old son. Exactly that. He would have forced the pills down her throat. I looked at the pathologist's report, and it was noted that she had a broken front tooth, but he reckoned she was drunk and broke it herself.'

'Sounds like he forced the bottle down her throat,' Evans said.

'Yes, it does. Which means there were three deaths, all in the local vicinity, all in December 1990.'

Dunbar looked over at Harry. *Should we share info with him?* Harry nodded. If Whitman hadn't been a retired detective, they wouldn't have.

'We were reading reports from around here. Twelve women were found dead over the years. Maybe they're women who this guy abducted.'

'Why do you call him Infinity?' Harry asked.

Whitman looked at him. 'Anybody got a glass of water? I take medication. Bloody heart problems.'

Vern got him a glass. 'Sorry about throwing you around.'

Whitman took out a small orange container, popped a tablet and washed it down. 'Don't worry about it. You thought you was dealing with a psychopath.'

They waited for him to carry on.

'It was just a name I came up with on my own. Nobody else knows I call him that. It all came about when I was looking at the photos of the dead women. The local plod took photos, thank God, and I requested to see them. And they accommodated me. The more photos I looked at, the more I saw a pattern emerging. Round the hands.'

'What sort of pattern?' Harry asked.

'On the curve between the thumb and the index finger there was a cut on one of the girls. You wouldn't even look at it twice, and I didn't either. Until I saw the second one. Then on a third, there was a cut along the edge of the index finger and one along the thumb. I didn't know it at first, but he posed the hand, because I saw it again later in a different photo. The hand was put into a fist, with the thumb across the index finger. With a little bit of a stretch, the two lines make an X.'

'That is a little bit of a stretch,' Dunbar said.

'Until you take one letter C, then take another one and invert it, and put the X in the middle. Join them up, you have the symbol for infinity.'

Evans had taken a notebook out and drawn the letters. He showed Dunbar the infinity symbol.

'What does this mean in relation to our killer?' Dunbar asked.

'I have no idea. It's just the way my mind works. It might be nothing at all, and it probably isn't or else somebody else would have spotted it.'

'Did you tell anybody else about this?' Harry asked.

'I did. Me old boss. He laughed at me. Told me I was burnt-out. Said he would be the bleedin' laughin' stock upstairs if he went to them with this. I didn't talk about it again.'

Dunbar sat back in his chair and tilted his head back for a moment, stretching his neck.

'Let me get this straight: this killer, and let's just call him Infinity for the sake of clarity, he comes back here when the Christmas Land fair is on, kills three women and then...what? Leaves? Kills somewhere else? And why did he kill the young woman the other day? Because she got away the first time?'

'That's exactly it,' said Whitman. 'Two other women were killed. She was attacked but got away. Now he kills her.'

'Why now?' Evans said. 'Why six years later?'

But they knew. Or they thought they knew.

'Martin Blair just got out of the hospital,' Dunbar said. 'He found the first one, didn't find the second one. Now he's back and a third one is killed, all of them friends. He's too young to have killed the women back in the day. He's thirty, which make him only just born when the killings started.'

'True. I don't think he's the killer, but I think he's connected somehow, maybe even without him realising it,' Whitman said.

'How come you were near Carol when she was murdered?' Harry asked.

'Because I was following her. She was at Christmas Land and I was there, keeping an eye on her. I thought he would go for her. Then I lost sight of her. I looked all around, then when I went to the edge of the market, I saw her going into the woods and somebody was in front of her. She was going in as if she knew her killer. By the time I got there, she was hanging from the tree.'

'There was blood on the trail.'

'Not from me. I tried to get her down, but then I heard the dog coming and I took off. I didn't think they would believe me and I can't afford to be locked up. I need to be out here helping you people. I'm retired. Nobody gives a shit about the killings because they don't know they're happening. Yes, you lot do, but if you don't solve this case, it will go cold, just like the others, and he'll lay low, coming here every Christmas and making deaths look like accidents. He'll never get caught. This is my last chance to catch him.'

'There's something different in your pattern,'

Harry said. 'If Carol was the third friend who was murdered six years later, then she's the last one, not the first one.'

'Two trains of thought here. One, he waited six years because he wanted to involve Martin Blair and he killed her to end that cycle. Two, he just killed her because in his mind he has OCD and he has to end it. Get it out of the way. Now he's going to start a new cycle.'

'Why is he leaving it so late in the month to do it?' Harry asked.

'Oh, sorry, I forgot to mention that. He kills between Christmas and New Year. Which means if we discount Carol, then three women are going to die this week.'

TWENTY-SEVEN

Harry had just poured himself a coffee when he got the phone call. He answered it and looked at Jimmy Dunbar and shook his head.

'What do you mean, not there?' He listened again before hanging up.

'What's wrong, Harry?' Dunbar asked.

'It's Alex. She's missing.'

Dunbar and Evans were on their feet in a split second. 'What do you mean?'

'That's all they would say on the phone. I have to go over there.'

'Where are you staying?' Dunbar asked Whitman.

'A little hotel on Main Street.'

'Give Muckle your mobile number. We need to keep in touch. And don't go doing anything stupid. It might get you killed.' Dunbar turned to Harry and Evans. 'Let's go.'

Harry gave Whitman his warrant card back.

The drive to the hospital took ten minutes. None of them talked on the short trip, except for Harry thinking out loud: 'How the hell can she be missing?'

Dunbar stopped near the front of the hospital and Harry walked up to the front desk.

'I'm DCI Harry McNeil. I got a call from Dr Carter.'

'He's expecting you. He'll meet you on the second floor.'

They took the lift up and Carter was waiting outside a small room that was designated for telling relatives that their loved one wasn't leaving the hospital alive. There were two little couches and some framed prints on the wall. Later on, Harry would remember one, a vase with flowers in it.

'Please, sit down,' Carter said, a grim look on his face.

'I don't want to fucking sit down,' Harry said.

Carter looked at the three men and decided it might be better if he were the one sitting.

'I can't explain what happened. Your wife was wheeled down to the radiology department for her scan and the porter left her there. When the radiologist came out, Mrs McNeil was gone.'

'Gone? I don't understand this. Fucking gone? What does that even mean?'

'There was no sign of her. The wheelchair she was taken downstairs in was found round the back in the staff car park.'

'Somebody took her?' Dunbar said, starting to get pissed off at the man's touchy-feely voice.

'We're not sure. I mean, she might have wheeled herself out and left.'

'Don't talk pish,' Dunbar said. 'Is her stuff still in her room? Her clothes and personal belongings?'

'They are. She had her phone with her. The porter saw it in her lap when he wheeled her down.'

'The porter? He was the last one to see her?'

'He was.'

'Where is the bastard?' Harry said.

'Let's not jump to conclusions. He wheeled her down, then he was back on the ward five minutes later.'

'Oh, fucking barry,' Evans said. 'That gave him time to wheel her out to his car, stick her in the boot and come back in.'

'Now, look, we can't go accusing anybody of anything,' Carter said.

'Give us five minutes with the cunt and we'll find out for sure if he did something to her,' Dunbar said.

'Now listen here –'

Dunbar put a hand up. 'Cut the righteous shite

out. You're on a hiding to nothing here, pal. You lost not only a patient but one of us. His wife. If I were you, I'd be worrying about whether I still had a career or not.'

'What about cameras?' Harry said.

'We don't have them inside,' said Carter. 'Only at the front door. The back door isn't covered. The staff car park isn't covered. We don't have a lot of crime here.'

Dunbar turned to Evans. 'Get on the phone and get this place swarming with uniforms. Everybody they can spare. I want witness statements, anything that might shed some light on what happened here.'

Evans nodded and left the room.

Harry took out his phone and called Alex's number. It went to voicemail. 'Alex, if you can hear this, I love you. I'm coming for you.'

He felt cold and numb. 'Why would anybody take her? Up here, in this pissant town?'

'I've already told staff that they have to cooperate in any way possible with you,' Carter said.

'I want to speak to that porter,' Dunbar said.

Carter nodded and left the room.

'Why, Jimmy? Why would somebody take her?'

'I think we know why, pal. Something to do with this case. They're warning us off. I've seen it before.'

'Did it end well?'

'Luckily, it did. But the DI running the case ended up leaving the force. His confidence was shot.'

'I'm not running away from this,' said Harry. 'If that fucking Blair family has anything to do with this, I'll take them all out and they can shove this job.'

Carter came back with the big porter.

'This is Lewis.'

'Sorry to hear about your wife, sir. I swear to God, I just took her down to the radiology department and left her there. There was nobody else about. I got back in the lift and came back up here.'

'Nobody else at all?'

'Only one of the domestic staff. She was in the lift and came out with a cart full of sheets.'

'What did she look like?'

'Dark hair. I didn't get a look at her face. She had a huge pile of towels on top of the sheets and had one arm up supporting it. It looked like it was going to tumble. She could hardly see over the top.'

'Hiding her face,' Dunbar said. 'Did you see her again?'

'No, just that one time. But to be honest, we're so busy taking patients to departments and picking them up again, I didn't think about it again.'

'Thanks, son. If you remember anything else, give us a shout.'

'Will do.' Lewis stopped before he left the room. 'Am I in trouble?'

'No. This wasn't your fault,' Dunbar answered.

Harry hoped he wouldn't have to come back and ask this man what his wife's last words had been.

Lewis left.

'You said you had security cameras at the front of the hospital,' Dunbar said.

Carter nodded.

'Take me to your security office.'

'I'm not sure of the legality,' Carter replied.

'Maybe I'm not making myself clear, son, because I come from Glasgow and people think we have a strong accent, so I'm going to speak slowly for your benefit. Take me to that fucking office now...or you'll be lucky if you can write a prescription for Smarties by the time I'm finished with you. And that man there? He's the one who will do the physical stuff.'

'Is that a threat?'

'Heid first down the stairs or oot a fucking window. That'll be your next move.'

'Jesus. Is that how they operate where you come from? Acting like thugs?'

'Now you're fucking getting it. Back home, I have to deal with a lot of hard bastards who would eat you for breakfast. Security office. Now.'

Carter tutted and led them out and along a corridor. Evans followed them down to the main level just as the first of the uniforms arrived, including Sergeant Lamb.

'Make sure he goes nowhere,' Dunbar instructed, pointing to Carter. 'And round up the domestic staff. We're looking for one with long, dark hair who took linens down to the back of the building.'

In the security office, two men were there, one watching the monitors, the other on the phone.

'There's no sign of her, sir,' the older one said.

'Pull up the footage from the front,' Harry said. 'Around the time my wife went missing. Anything coming from the staff car park round the back.'

'Absolutely. We were told she went missing around ten-ish. I'll start from nine forty-five and see what we've got.'

The three detectives watched the main monitor like they were watching Scotland live in the World Cup final. A truck came round from the back with a food service company name on the side. Fast-forward to just after ten and another truck came out. This time it was a linen company.

'Stop there,' Harry said. 'Zoom in.'

The company logo was clearly visible.

Dunbar turned to Evans. 'Call and see who was driving that vehicle.'

'Sir.' Evans left the office.

'Roll the tape again,' Harry said.

The truck left the car park, and a few minutes later a hearse left.

'Thanks.' Harry turned to Dunbar. 'I want that Lewis guy to show us where he left Alex.'

Dunbar looked at the security man. 'Can you get in touch with him? Porter named Lewis.'

'Aye, no bother. They carry walkies on them.' He put out the message and Lewis got back to him.

'Security office need you, pal.'

Five minutes later, Lewis was in the office.

'Show us where you left Mrs McNeil.'

'Absolutely. This way.' He led them out into the corridor and along to the lifts. Evans followed them.

Dunbar waved a uniform over. 'Come with us.'

'The driver's back at the warehouse,' said Evans. 'He filled up with this load and went straight back. Other workers unloaded the baskets. Then the driver went out again.'

'Right, Robbie. Go and track him down. He might have seen something.'

Evans nodded and left.

TWENTY-EIGHT

Downstairs, Lewis showed Harry and Dunbar where he had wheeled Alex to and left her.

'This is the spot. They sit along from the door, so they don't get bumped by somebody getting wheeled out, and then the tech comes out and gets them. They're notified when a patient is coming down, so they know somebody is waiting.'

Dunbar turned to the uniform. 'Speak with the tech.' To Lewis: 'Man or woman?'

'Woman.'

To the uniform again. 'Ask her what she saw when she came out to get Mrs McNeil.'

The uniform went into the radiology suite.

'Show us what's down here,' Harry said, pointing to a corridor at the end of this one. It bent round to the right and disappeared from view.

'It's the mortuary down here,' Lewis said, and Harry got a sudden bad feeling in his gut.

They walked down, nobody else around, their footsteps echoing off the walls. This corridor was dimly lit. They followed it down, Harry beginning to have the feeling he always got when he went to a mortuary.

They turned left and the corridor was brighter here. A door with a security bar was on the right-hand side.

'That leads to the staff car park,' Lewis said.

They walked past it and turned left into a short corridor with a set of rubber doors. They went through and the antiseptic smell was strong.

'This is the mortuary.'

Dunbar nodded. 'We came in through the back door and spoke to a young lassie, Stacey,' he said.

'She's nice. Old Doc Hamilton is a pain, though.' Lewis kept his voice down.

As if by magic, Stacey Nichols came round. 'Hello again.' She smiled at them but then saw how serious they were. 'Anything wrong?'

'One of our officers is missing,' Dunbar said. 'Last seen along at radiology.'

'Oh my God. What's happened? Is it the nice young bloke you were with?'

'No, it's my wife,' said Harry. 'You met her the other night.'

'Oh God. That's awful.'

'If she was brought along here by somebody, how easy would it have been for them to get her out?' Dunbar asked.

'She wasn't kicking and screaming, that's for sure, or I would have heard. I know we play the radio in there sometimes, but if there was anybody struggling, that would have got our attention.' She thought for a moment. 'There are always domestics coming down here. They go along that little corridor there to the roller door. A truck backs up and takes the stuff away. Like in, oh, I don't know what they're called, but big laundry baskets on wheels. Somebody could have been in one.'

'We have somebody going to talk to the linen company driver right now.'

'He comes late morning for our stuff. He brings fresh laundry and takes the dirty stuff away,' Stacey said.

'Any of the staff leave here?'

'Not that I know of. What time was it around?'

'Ten,' Harry said.

'No. The boys went out to a sudden death earlier, but they were back before nine with the body. Then there was Anderson Birrell. He came with a hearse and took a body away. I have the paperwork. Sorry I couldn't be more helpful.'

'You've been more than helpful.' Harry put a hand on her arm, more to steady himself than anything else.

'You okay?' she asked just as Dunbar stepped in and took Harry by the arm.

'I'm fine. I just haven't eaten this morning.'

'I've got him, hen.'

'Look, bring him into the office and get him seated,' said Stacey.

'I'll be fine,' Harry said, but the room swam for a moment.

'We know how you Edinburgh softies like to sit down and have a cup of tea every five minutes,' Dunbar said.

They went into a small office.

'Dr Hamilton is out on a call with the boys and the van,' said Stacey. 'She'll be a while. Let me get the kettle on.'

'You don't have to go to that trouble,' Harry said.

'No trouble. I'll make us a brew. I was going on break anyway. I can give you tea, but wouldn't you know it, the greedy old sod has eaten all the biscuits again.'

'Dr Hamilton doesn't look like the kind who would fill herself up on biscuits,' Dunbar said.

'No, not her, old Doc Renfrew. He eats our biscuits.'

'Who's Renfrew?' Dunbar asked. He and Harry looked at her.

'He used to be the pathologist here, apparently, until he had a heart attack. You'd think he would know better. He's only sixty, Dr Hamilton said. He looks a lot older. Obviously, he doesn't look after himself. I've only been here a couple of months, so I didn't work with him. He's only up here for Christmas and New Year. He lives down south now. But he can't keep away from the place. I mean, he was in here this morning and all the bloody biscuits are gone.'

'How long ago was he the pathologist?'

'He retired six months ago.'

TWENTY-NINE

Alex jolted awake as the smell got sucked into her nostrils.

The man was standing over her, something in his hand. 'You're just inhaling ammonia and your body is reacting to it, making you suck in fresh oxygen, which jolts you awake. Otherwise known as smelling salts. About time you were coming round, lazy cow.'

'Where...what...?' Alex struggled to get the words out. He was wearing a ski mask and she could only see his eyes and mouth.

'*Where* doesn't matter. You're quite safe, I promise you. The *what* part of your question...well, need-to-know basis, I'm afraid. And right now, you don't need to know.'

Alex's mind was clearing and she realised that her

left wrist was handcuffed to the metal bedpost. She looked at it.

'Yes, I'm sorry about that, in your condition and all, but needs must. You can sit up or lie down, it's your choice. You'll be able to eat and watch some TV if you like, but you have to stay handcuffed to the bedframe. I'm not going to hurt you, I promise you that. You're just a tiny pawn in what is turning out to be a big game.'

'What's going on? I was in the hospital. How did I get here?'

'No, don't you worry your pretty little head about things. You were given a little sedative, nothing that will harm your baby, and I made sure you were comfortable while you were being transported here.'

The room was warm and she heard a log fire crackling in the small fireplace. The curtains had been opened and she could see daylight. Grey sky. That was it.

'Are we still in Blairgowan?' she asked. Her mouth was dry and she was finding it hard to speak.

The man left the room and came back with a tray with food on it. 'Chicken soup, glass of water and some nausea medication. I know you don't trust me, but the meds are there if the sickness becomes unbearable. And think about how you can't leave the bed; if you're sick, you'll have to lie in it. The meds will help. If I wanted to harm you, I would have done it when you were unconscious.'

He put the tray on the bed on the side that she was handcuffed. 'I have to warn you, though: if you decide to throw the soup at me, you'll get no more food. You won't get toilet privileges. There's a little en-suite there that you can use. But again, any funny business and no more toilet. Do you understand?'

'Yes.'

'Right. Have a glass of water. It will make you feel better.'

'I'm not drinking that,' she replied.

'Still don't trust me. Here, let me show you.' He took the glass and had a drink from it. 'There. I wouldn't poison myself now, would I?'

He left and she drank the water. Then she reached over herself and slid the tray closer. She was famished now. She grabbed the bowl of soup and managed to get it across and down onto the cover without spilling it. The soup tasted good. From a can, but still.

She ate it up, focusing on the little TV, its screen blank. She was about to call him when she felt the tiredness kick in. Her eyes were getting heavier and all the light was being sucked from the room.

Then she realised, just before she closed her eyes.

He'd drugged the soup.

THIRTY

'I was just thinking,' Gary Whitman said. He was still in the kitchen and Vern was pottering about.

'Oh yeah? That can be dangerous.'

Whitman laughed. 'You know how the hearse was crashed into the church? What if that wasn't an accident?'

'What do you mean?'

'Well, I was working a case once where a guy was abducting women and he was taunting us. He crashed a car into a shop. Turned out he had taken a woman who used to work there. He crashed it just enough to draw attention but not to hurt himself. That got me thinking: what if...? I was going to go over there today and have a little nose around. You up for it?'

'I'm not sure that's a good idea.'

'Not with me. I mean with the big fella. I'm bleedin' knackered now.'

She thought about it some more. She had given thought to maybe joining the police, making a career of it in Glasgow. Working alongside Robbie Evans wouldn't be so bad.

Just then, Muckle came in with Sparky.

'Sparky my boy!' Whitman said, holding his arms out. Sparky wagged his tail and rushed over to the man, who rubbed the side of his head. 'I was just saying to Vern here that maybe this nut job crashed the hearse into the church on purpose, to draw our attention to there. I've seen it happen before. Maybe you should go and have a look.'

Muckle looked at Vern. 'What do you think?'

'I think we have time to do this before we have to go on duty. Where's Shug?'

'At home with David. He won't be in until it's time to work. But let's go. I'm bored already.'

'I hope you don't mind if I don't join you,' said Whitman. 'My sciatica is killing me. Being rugby-tackled didn't do me back any good.'

'Sorry about that,' Vern said.

'Don't you worry your head about that. You was doing what had to be done. I wouldn't mind just going back to me hotel. Stretch me back out a bit.'

'Sure. We can meet up later.'

They left the house and got into one of the old Range Rovers that belonged to the estate, Sparky relegated to the back of the car. Muckle drove round to where the hearse had been chased and carefully negotiated the road until he came to the little lane and drove down it. The snow was coming down slowly again, gradually filling in the tyre tracks from all the vehicles that had come down here, including the tow truck that had taken the hearse away.

Muckle stopped the car and Sparky sensed something was going on and started yelping in the back.

'Sparks, enough. You'll make me fuckin' deef.' Muckle looked at Vern. 'Pardon the French.'

She just smiled at him. 'Come on, Sparky, time for work,' she said, and the dog turned towards the back. She opened it up and let him out, grabbing his lead and handing him over to Muckle.

The snow was coming down harder now.

'Girls were found dead in this cemetery here,' Muckle said. 'It goes some way to the back.'

'We can split up,' Vern said.

'There's a nutter on the loose,' Muckle said.

'I think I can take care of myself, Muckle.'

'Okay, okay, have it your way. I'll take him way back there. The walk will do him good. Come on, boy.'

Muckle walked past the side of the old church and he and the dog were soon out of sight as a high wind whipped up the ground snow, making it look like a blizzard.

Vern walked past some of the debris from the smashed hearse and stood looking at the door to the church. For an abandoned building it was in decent shape, structurally. She reached out and turned the old doorknob, expecting the hinges on the door to creak, but they moved silently.

She took out the small torch from her belt and shone it around. It was dusty and cold and there were cobwebs everywhere.

She walked forward and the floorboards creaked alarmingly, but they held. The pulpit was straight ahead. Vern wondered when a minister had last held a service from up there.

The windows were still intact, if caked with dirt, but a gloomy light fell through them. Wind whistled through gaps somewhere, but still this place felt a few degrees warmer than outside.

She moved forward until she came to the first line of pews. Then she saw it.

A woman hanging from the rafters.

Vern's breath caught in her throat, but she composed herself. She ran forward, bracing herself, and saw the chair tipped over underneath the woman's feet.

Christ, had she hanged herself?

She righted the chair, stood on it, grabbed hold of the woman and pulled a knife from her pocket, then tried to take the weight and cut the rope at the same time. The knife was small, but it was doing the trick.

Then, all of a sudden, she sensed movement near her, and the chair was kicked out from under her.

She fell hard, landing on her back, and felt the air rush out of her lungs just as the black shadow was on top of her. She tried to bring the knife up but realised it had flown from her hand as she tried to save herself.

There was a sharp pain in her neck, and then her eyes closed.

'Come on, boy, there's nowt here. Let's go and see if Vern's found anything,' Muckle said to the dog. Sparky got confused for a moment and stood waiting for Muckle to throw a snowball. Muckle ignored him, but his boots kicked up the powdery snow and as it flew up Sparky tried to bite it.

'Aw, come on, this is difficult enough, ya daft bastard.'

Still the dog played as they approached the church – then he stopped and stood still, staring at the old building. The fur on his back went up and he started growling.

Muckle got a bad feeling.

'Come on, boy, let's go see Vern.' He started running through the deep snow as best he could, with Sparky pulling on his lead. The snow thinned out as they got to the car park, and Muckle had his baton out as the dog pulled him into the church. There was no way of making a covert entrance with the dog barking now.

Muckle stopped short when he saw the woman hanging there. He took his phone out, Sparky going berserk. He tried to hold the baton in his left hand while he dialled a number with his right.

'Vern! You here?' he shouted. She should have shown herself by now.

The phone was answered at the other end.

'It's Muckle. You need to get to the old church. We have another one.'

THIRTY-ONE

Dunbar was standing out in the corridor. He called David, Shug's husband.

'Dave, it's Jimmy Dunbar. I need to know how good you are on that computer of yours.'

'I like to think I'm the best, but there are people who would probably argue with that.'

'How good are you at doing searches on people?'

'Ever heard of taking sweets from a baby?'

'I need you to run a name. Albert Renfrew. He lived here in town until six months ago when he had a heart attack and moved down south. He was a pathologist. He retired from Blairgowan hospital.'

'I'll get on it now. Call you when I'm done.'

'Good man.'

Harry came out of the office. 'You think it's the same guy?'

'Don't you? Some light bulbs are going off in my head. He retired six months ago. He's come up here at Christmas. He's a friend of Dr Hamilton's, so he can weasel his way in here to find out what they know.'

'Bastard. Why didn't we know about him before?'

'He didn't do anything stupid to put himself on our radar before. But if he's taken Alex, then he's put himself front and centre.'

'We should ask Carter what he knows about Renfrew.'

'Let's get back upstairs and ask him now.'

They walked back along the corridor and Dunbar's phone rang. It was Evans.

'Get back here, Robbie. We have a new lead, somebody we didn't know about. I'll tell you when you get here.'

He hung up and they took the lift to the ground floor and went back to the security office.

'Can you call Dr Carter for us?' said Dunbar. 'I need to speak to him urgently.'

'Dr Carter left a wee while ago. He said he wasn't feeling well and that he would see you later.'

'Does he live in town here?'

'On the outskirts. In one of the big houses on the new estate.'

'Can you give us his address?'

'HR would have to do that. I mean, they're sticklers

179

for policies. I think you might have to get a warrant for that.'

'Alright, son, we'll follow the rules.'

They left the office again and Dunbar made a call.

'David? Sorry to be a pain, but I need some more info, if you can manage it.'

'I'm only too happy to help a friend of Shug's. He says hi, but he's away to get ready for work.'

Dunbar told David what he needed.

'Stay on the line. That's so easy I could do it in my sleep.'

'I bet Carter's packing his suitcase now. He's fucked up big time and I bet he's on the run,' Harry said, getting agitated.

'What if he's working with this Renfrew joker? Maybe he helped Renfrew. Got Alex down to radiology so Renfrew could grab her.'

Dunbar's phone rang and he answered it, thinking it was David. It was Muckle. Dunbar listened before hanging up.

'Muckle's at the old church where the hearse crashed. Another woman's been hanged. He's calling it in. We have to get round there.'

'I have to go see Carter. I have to know if he's involved.'

'You can't do that, Harry. You might do something stupid.'

'I'm going, Jimmy.'

'Okay, I can't stop you, but I'm sending Robbie with you.'

'Okay, fine.'

'Meet me over at the church later.'

Just then, Evans came marching in.

'Don't get comfortable,' Dunbar told him. 'Harry will explain on the way.'

THIRTY-TWO

Harry and Evans were sitting in the big Land Rover waiting for Dunbar's call.

'Jesus, sir, I'm gutted about Alex. If I get my hands on the bastard...'

'Me first, Robbie.'

Harry's phone rang and Dunbar gave him the address that David had acquired. Evans put the address into Google Maps and they left the hospital car park.

'This pathologist has just gone to the top of our list,' Harry said after explaining what had gone down in the mortuary.

'How did he get Alex out if he took her?'

'I don't know yet.'

They drove along Main Street before taking a left and heading out of town. They were going up into the hills when they found the street they were looking for. Evans slowed down and they started looking at house numbers. They were old properties fronted by high hedges and thick stone walls. They obviously valued their privacy here, even in the middle of nowhere.

'There. Number thirty-nine,' Evans said, pointing. A BMW X5 sat in the driveway. Harry wondered if there was gravel under all the snow. Two trails led to the wheels.

'Let's go and see if he's in,' Harry said as Evans parked behind the BMW, blocking it in.

They got out and walked through the snow on the pathway. It was coming down more heavily now and Harry pulled his collar up against the cold, wet flakes.

He banged hard against the solid wood.

No answer.

He tried again, stamping his feet, not so much from the cold but from the adrenalin running through his body. He banged louder and they waited, but still nothing.

Evans walked over to the bay window and put his hands up against the glass, peering in. The curtains were drawn, but there was a gap at the bottom.

'Sir, we need to get in. Carter's slumped over on his settee.'

Harry started kicking the door, but it was solid and didn't budge. Evans took out his extendable baton and smashed the living room window, having to break through both panes of glass in the double glazing; even in old houses you needed to keep the draughts out. He broke the glass all around the window frame, knocking the little shards out, and kept his baton in one hand as he climbed through. He pulled the curtains apart, throwing light into the room, and Harry could see the doctor lying on his side.

Evans walked over to the man as Harry climbed through. His entry wasn't quite as dignified as Evans had been, but he got the job done.

He stood looking at Carter, at the open, empty eyes.

At the needle in his arm.

'He's well deid,' Evans said. 'I'll call it in.'

'Where's my wife, you bastard?' Harry asked the dead man.

THIRTY-THREE

'Well, well, the gang's all here,' said Gibson, the scene of crime chief, as he pulled his white suit up. 'Maybe you could go inside and help fuck up the crime scene, just like that big gawk with the radge dug. I thought he would have known better, being an ex-copper.'

'He went through some tough shite in his job as a copper, not working in fucking Trumpton like you. He knows exactly what he's doing. I just hope the same can be said for you.'

'I'm the best there is round here.'

'Then we're all fucked, aren't we?'

Dunbar closed the door of the patrol car he'd come in and walked away. The snow was blowing across the cemetery, making him squint his eyes. Half of him wanted to trample around more than he had to, just to piss off the forensics man, but he kept it professional.

Inside the old church, Sparky was growling at a big uniform who looked like he ate a couple of cabers for breakfast.

'Go and watch the door, son,' Dunbar said, and the uniform nodded.

'For a big bastard, he's fairly sweating,' Dunbar said to Muckle. Sparky relaxed when he saw who it was.

More suited techs were photographing the body. Dunbar looked over.

'Any idea who it is, son?' he asked.

'Not a clue,' said Muckle.

The dead woman's long blonde hair had fallen down, covering her face.

Then Dunbar had an idea. 'You took photos of the dead girl who was found the other day?' he asked the tech with the camera.

'I did, yes.'

'I don't suppose they're on the card in your camera there?'

'They are indeed. We make multiple copies back at the lab of course, but yes, they're on here.'

'Can you show me some? Particularly of her hands if you took any.'

'I did. Hands, face, neck, the rope. You name it, I took a photo of it.'

'Just go to her hands.'

The tech moved through the photos, looking at the

little screen on the back of the camera, until he got to photos of Carol's hands.

Dunbar held one side of the camera and scrolled through. 'How do you zoom in?'

The tech pressed a button.

'Just to her thumb.' Dunbar looked at it. 'Next thumb.'

The tech zoomed back out and moved the photos along and then did the same thing.

'Thanks,' said Dunbar. 'That's all I need.'

'Right, chappies, let's see what we've got,' Gibson said, marching down the aisle like he was late for a wedding.

'He's too cheery for this job. Maybe we should take a look at him,' Dunbar said. His phone rang again. 'I swear to Christ, my life was a lot easier before these things.' He answered it, listened and hung up.

'That was Harry,' he told Muckle. 'They found Dr Carter dead.'

'Who?'

'Never mind.' He looked at Muckle. 'You alright, pal?'

'Vern wasn't here when I got back. I'm still waiting for her to meet me here. We were checking this place out. She's usually punctual, and I thought she would have come running when she saw all the commotion.'

'God, you don't think...?'

'I'm trying not to think, Jimmy. That's the problem. There's no sign of her.'

'Give it a few minutes. I'm not going to insult your intelligence and ask if you called her.'

'Voicemail.'

Dunbar filled Muckle in on what had happened, not sure if he had already told him some of it.

They watched as the techs dragged a pew over a bit towards the corpse. One stood on it and reached up to the rope to cut it. They laid her gently down, showing her respect in death. Gibson reached down and gently pushed the hair away from the woman's face.

'Christ Almighty,' he said, standing up.

Dunbar and Muckle walked over.

'Who is it?' Dunbar asked, but then he looked down and saw for himself.

The pathologist, Dr Valerie Henderson.

He stood up straight. 'I think we just had our theory confirmed. Albert Renfrew was having tea and biscuits with Henderson at the mortuary this morning.'

'Do you think that's how he left the hospital? In her car?' said Muckle. 'But where would Alex have been? In the boot? Maybe he forced her.'

'That would make sense, but something isn't adding up here,' said Dunbar. 'First of all, why would Carter kill himself?'

'You said Renfrew was having tea with Henderson in the office?' Muckle said. 'What car did he come in?'

'I don't know how he got there.'

'He must have just parked in the public car park.'

'No,' said Dunbar. 'That lassie said he comes in through the staff entrance like he still owns the place. Maybe he got a lift.'

'I think he took Vern as well as Alex.'

'Come and have a look at this!' a uniform shouted. He was at the end of the platform where the pulpit was. And he'd opened a trapdoor.

THIRTY-FOUR

Alex slowly woke up again. Her head was pounding this time and her mouth was dry. The light from the dirty window was almost blinding. She tried moving her left arm again, but it was still firmly locked to the bed. It was feeling cramped and sore, so she tried moving up closer to the head of the bed to see if that would ease the discomfort.

Then she noticed the person lying on the bed next to hers. A woman dressed in black. Her face seemed familiar, but Alex couldn't put a name to the face. The woman's right hand was handcuffed to the brass bedframe. She was stirring as if having a nightmare, moaning and making weird noises. Then, after a while, she opened her eyes. Looked at Alex.

'I know you,' she said, her voice barely a whisper. 'I...can't remember who you are.'

'Alex. Harry's wife.' Then it clicked who this woman was. 'You're Vern, Muckle's friend.'

'Where the hell are we? What happened?'

'I was taken from the hospital. I don't know about you.'

Vern looked up at the ceiling, willing her mind to start working. Then something clicked in her head. 'I was in the old church. There was a woman hanging. I climbed on a chair to try to get her down, but then the chair was kicked from out beneath me and I fell. Then...I woke up here.'

'Who was it? The woman?' Alex asked.

'I don't know. I didn't see her face before I fell.'

'I think we might be next on his list. Whoever he is.'

Vern took a couple of deep breaths. 'We caught the guy who was creeping about where Carol was found. Did Harry tell you?'

'No. Who is he?'

'He's a cop from the Met. He's known about this killer for thirty years. Nobody believed him, or they dismissed it out of hand. He calls the killer Infinity. Long story.'

'I'm not going anywhere,' Alex said, giving the handcuff another yank just for good measure.

THIRTY-FIVE

Dunbar walked over. 'What the hell is that?'

Part of the platform had swung open to reveal a set of stairs that descended into darkness. Everybody in the church looked round.

'Don't just stand there, son – get your arse down there and see what it's all about.'

The uniform hesitated.

'Out the way,' Dunbar said to the big man. He took his phone out and switched the little torch on. 'Muckle! With me.'

'I'll go down first with the dog.' Muckle led the way, shining a little torch in front of him.

'Right, some of you lot get over here,' Dunbar said to the uniforms. 'We're going down here.'

The big uniform went down the stairs after Muckle, Dunbar next, then a couple more uniforms.

They all had their batons out, and it was at this point that Dunbar wished the police in Scotland were armed. He for one would be quite happy to be armed.

At the bottom of the stairs there was a large room. As Muckle shone his light around, Sparky growled. The torchlight illuminated a string hanging from a bulb, so Muckle pulled it. The light above his head sprang to life, together with lights around the room.

It was a storage area, with old furniture leaning against a wall. But it was the row of coffins sitting over to one side that caught everybody's attention.

'Christ, they're old,' Dunbar said.

Muckle walked over to them, his eyes focused on the lid of the first one. Then he turned to Dunbar. 'What if he put Alex in here?'

'It's dusty. It's been here a long time.'

'I know that, Jimmy. But see the finger marks on the edge,' Muckle said. 'It's been opened recently.'

Dunbar didn't have an answer. He counted the coffins; six of them.

Over on the far wall was a workshop area with woodworking tools. There was a lot of sawdust on the floor and cans of varnish lying around. Strips of material lay discarded.

'What does this look like to you, Muckle?' Dunbar asked.

Muckle just stared at the coffin with the finger marks on it. 'I don't know.'

'We've both heard of unscrupulous funeral directors who've taken bodies out of expensive coffins and put them into cheap wooden ones for the cremation, then repurposed the coffins. It looks to me like somebody's got this scam going.'

'They're dusty, so maybe he doesn't do it often.'

Dunbar ran a finger over one of the coffins. 'It's sawdust, pal. What if they sand them down and give them a different colour, just in case?'

'These aren't that old then.' Muckle looked at the last two coffins, in the corner. They didn't look new and they had cobwebs over them. 'That's not sawdust.'

Dunbar moved over to them. They were old and hadn't been touched in years. He gripped the edge of a coffin lid and opened it.

'Jesus,' he said, looking into it.

THIRTY-SIX

The decomposed remains of a woman lay in the coffin. Dunbar's heart was beating way faster than was safe for a man of his age.

'I wonder who this is?' Muckle said.

'Caitlin McGhee went missing thirty years ago, along with two of her friends. I'm guessing this is one of them.'

Muckle squeezed between this coffin and the other old one and opened the lid. Another female. Decomposed.

'This could be the other one.'

Dunbar turned to one of the uniforms. 'Get Gibson down here.'

The uniform almost sprinted back up the stairs, before reluctantly coming back down with the forensics man.

'Fucking touching stuff, I suppose,' Gibson said. He kept away from Sparky.

'Have a look at those two coffins,' Dunbar said.

Gibson moved forward and looked into each of the coffins. 'Just like the one from the hearse.'

'Could they have been dead for thirty years?' Muckle asked.

'I would say so. If that's the timeframe you're looking at, then yes, they could have been dead for that amount of time. An expert will have a better idea, but this lowly forensics officer would say that would fit with the amount of decomposition.'

Gibson stepped back and looked around the subterranean room. 'Somebody's got a nice little side line going here. What have they been doing? Stripping coffins and re-lining them?'

'What gave it away?' Dunbar said. 'The lacquer or the satin material?'

'And here we go again with the shotgun wit. A blind man can see what's going on down here. Who do you think it is?'

'A funeral director maybe?'

Gibson shook his head, not rising to the bait. 'There's only one in this town – old, frosty Birrell. You'd get on well with him.'

'What about the new conglomerate?' Dunbar asked.

'What conglomerate? He's the only one who deals with death in this town.'

'That's not what he told DCI McNeil.'

The uniforms were looking around the room, chasing off the shadows with their torches. Dunbar stood looking at the coffins, trying to convince himself that he should open them, just to make sure.

He said a silent prayer and started opening the lids. The last coffin held a surprise.

'Muckle,' he said, shining his light into the coffin.

The dead face of Anderson Birrell looked back at them.

Gibson came over and had a look at the dead man. 'That's the funeral director's son. He doesn't look as if he's been dead that long.'

They could see a ligature around his neck.

'I need to make a phone call,' Dunbar said.

'This used to be a nice little church, but now the image is ruined,' Gibson said.

'Where do people go to worship now?' Muckle asked.

'The big church in town. This is the original church, built by the Blairs and the Gowans when they were starting this town. It got too small, though, so they built the new one, back in the seventies, I think. This one was still used up until around thirty years ago.'

Muckle looked at the man. 'People could go to worship at either church?'

'No, no, I mean this church was used by the Boy Scouts. From the camp.'

'What camp?'

'The one up the road. The Blair scouts' camp, up by the loch. It was a popular place, until those lassies went missing from there.'

'What lassies?' Muckle asked.

'You not paying attention?' Gibson nodded to the coffins. 'Those lassies. And the one in the hearse. They were last seen up at Camp Blair.'

THIRTY-SEVEN

Dunbar was outside talking on the phone when Muckle came out. 'David? It's Jimmy. Listen, can you do me a favour, pal? I'll make sure you get payment from Glasgow for your work.'

'Jimmy, all I ask in return is that you help me with some research for this book I'm planning. Ask anything you want.'

'Good job, son, I won't forget it. And of course I'll help you. Now, we just found two more bodies and we're thinking they're the other two girls who went missing. Can you do some research on that? Their names, anything about them?'

'I certainly can. And I can keep a copy for my book.'

'Terrific. Win-win.'

'I'll get back to you shortly. This shouldn't take me long.'

The snow was falling harder now, almost blinding. Headlights from the big Land Rover hit Dunbar's retinas before the car dipped down into the driveway. Robbie Evans and Harry got out and walked over to them.

Dunbar hung up. 'We discovered bodies in coffins down in the basement of the church,' he told Harry and Evans, and then explained exactly what they had found. He could see Harry tensing up.

'The girls who went missing all those years ago?'

'Yes. They were down in that basement. Two of them anyway. When we found that body in the coffin in the crashed hearse, we thought it was an accident. Now I don't know what the hell is going on.'

'No sign of Alex?' Evans asked.

'Nothing,' said Dunbar. 'I was thinking that maybe she'd been taken out in that hearse. But the funeral director is in one of the coffins down there.'

'Whoever killed him took the hearse?'

'Maybe he had taken Alex out in it,' Harry said and the words made him feel sick. If she had been taken out in it, had she still been alive at the time?

He couldn't picture it.

'Jimmy, that forensics guy told me about a scout camp near here,' Muckle said. 'The boys still used this church after the big one opened. It was just for them.'

Gibson came out of the church and Harry waved

him over. The forensics man looked across at Muckle, but he was watching Sparky, who had suddenly focused on Gibson.

'Tell us about the camp up the road.'

'I was there with the Boy Scouts when I was a boy. We had some good laughs, but the counsellors were a bit lacking. We would stay there for a couple of weeks in the summer, learning new skills. We loved it. We called it Camp Infinity. Then those girls went missing and it all went to fuck after that.'

'You called it what?' Dunbar said.

'Camp Infinity.'

'Why did you call it that?'

'It was like time was infinite. We loved it there, me and my pals. That's why we named it Camp Infinity.'

'Where exactly is it?' Dunbar asked.

'Easy. Just go up the road here, and as it bends round to the right, the camp entrance is over on your left. It's hard to see if you're not looking for it; most people are concentrating on not putting their car through a fucking hedge. But it's still there.'

'Thanks, Ewan,' Harry said.

Dunbar looked at Harry and Gibson. 'We're going up the road to have a look at some old camp.' Then to Muckle: 'Keep an eye on things here for me.'

'I can come with you, boss. Bring Sparky.'

'This is police business. I can't put you in danger.'

Muckle laughed. 'No disrespect, but bollocks. Alex is missing. Maybe Sparky can sense something. Or chew somebody. Don't worry about me.'

'Let him come, Jimmy,' Harry said. 'I'm getting desperate. I want to find Alex. I don't know where she is. I'm willing to try anything at this point.'

'Alright, son,' said Dunbar. 'Let's get going. Robbie, park your arse back in that driver's seat.'

As the others headed to the Land Rover, Dunbar waved a uniform over and told him where they were going. 'Get a patrol car and a couple of your colleagues and follow us up there.'

He got in the car and nobody said a word as Evans drove the car up the hill.

Even Sparky was quiet.

THIRTY-EIGHT

Wee Shug was getting ready for work while his husband was busy on the computer.

'Christmas Land is closing at nine on Hogmanay, so we can get to the party in plenty of time.'

'Magic. Is Vern going?'

'I suppose so. She seems to be getting on well with Robbie Evans.'

'She's nice. I was thinking of interviewing her for my book. I'd like to get different perspectives.' David smiled at Shug. 'I'm liking this idea more and more. It's something I'd really like to get into if I could make a living at it. I'll keep doing the IT work, though.'

'And we're still going to Glasgow?' Shug said.

'I'd like that. I mean, this place is okay, but it's a bit twee for me. I can't imagine living here all year round.

But I'll go wherever you go, obviously. We took our vows and I'm in this for the long haul.'

'I appreciate it. I might go back to the force. I mean, not everybody is homophobic like my old sergeant back on the island.'

'I would hope not. It is the twenty-first century after all.' David smiled at Shug and turned back to his computer.

'Besides, this place is bloody dangerous,' Shug said. 'Do you know how many people die here each year? Skiers, people falling down hills. Car crashes.'

'I know. I did some research for Jimmy. I think we'd be better off heading south.' David brought up the article that he'd saved and then did a web search. 'Look at this. When you do a search about people dying in the Highlands, there are tons of newspaper articles about it. It's like it's vying to be the most dangerous place in Britain.'

Then something caught his eye and he opened up the article.

'Oh, crap. This isn't right.'

'What is it?' Shug asked.

'This here.' David pointed to the screen. 'I need to call Jimmy Dunbar.'

THIRTY-NINE

Ewan Gibson was right. On the approach to the bend in the road, you kept your eyes looking ahead to make sure you made it round in one piece. So Dunbar kept his eyes on the left while Evans approached the bend.

'There it is,' Dunbar said, pointing. 'On the left. And slow this fucking thing down, Robbie. I don't want to be upside down, hanging from the seatbelt.'

'My granny doesn't panic like you. I'm barely doing the speed limit.'

'Aye, well, this is not the autobahn. Just be bloody careful.'

Evans made it into the old driveway without incident and he looked in the mirror and made a face at Dunbar.

The driveway was overgrown and nature had assaulted the sign for the camp many years ago. One thing that everybody noticed was the tyre marks in the snow.

'Sneaky bastard,' Harry said. 'How the hell did we not know about this place to begin with?'

Nobody had the answer.

Evans guided the car up the drive and they saw the first building appear in the distance.

'It doesn't show much on here,' Muckle said, looking at his phone, 'but there's a small loch at the top. Buildings are scattered about.'

They approached a hut with a window in it, an old security office.

'Fat lot of good that did,' Dunbar observed. 'Three lassies disappear and what were security doing, I wonder?'

'The camp counsellors were probably the security people. It's not as if they would have had proper patrols, just leaders,' Harry said.

'Whatever it was, they dropped the ball,' Evans said.

The big car made it to the top of a hill, the tyres crunching through the snow. Over on the left was a small amphitheatre with wooden benches built into the side of the hill, looking down. Further up, cabins were lined up facing the small loch. Snow was coming down but not as hard.

'The tracks in the snow go round to the left,' Evans said, following them.

They followed the road round and saw more cabins and a couple of houses. Looking through the trees, they saw more houses back there, higher up on a hill. Then the tyre tracks became one big jumbled mess.

Sparky jumped up, growling.

'Check those boards, boys,' said Dunbar. 'If any are loose, we'll get inside. Otherwise, we'll search those houses. I've got uniforms coming up.'

They got out and started pulling at the boards on the windows and the doors, but they were solid.

Harry looked around. He could see more cabins through the trees.

'This place is a lot bigger than I thought,' he said.

Muckle was looking at his phone. 'It says here they added the houses when they turned it into a ski resort. They rented the houses out in the winter, but it was the scout camp in the summer.'

'Alex could be anywhere,' Harry said, feeling the tension in him about to explode. 'She could have been taken anywhere.'

Sparky started growling and pulling on his lead. Muckle dropped his phone into the snow.

'Fuck's sake. Look at my phone, ya hoor. Just as well it fell in the snow.'

As Muckle bent down to pick it up, he looked up

the hill. And something caught his eye between the snowfall and the trees.

'Good boy,' he said. Then he turned to the others. 'I think we can narrow it down.'

He pointed up the hill and the others looked, moving their heads so they could see what he was pointing at.

'Unless it's a crashed UFO, I can see fuck all,' Dunbar said.

'I can,' Harry replied. 'Up there. Smoke.'

FORTY

They both heard the footsteps thumping up the stairs. The creak of the floorboards as he walked along the landing towards the room they were in. Then the latch opening and the hinges screeching as the door swung inward.

'Glad to see you're both awake,' said the man with the mask. 'We have visitors.'

Alex sat bolt upright, her left hand catching the bedpost. She could see the man's eyes but couldn't tell if he was angry or disappointed or scared. Maybe all three?

Then he laughed and she knew they were fucked.

'This is going to be fun. I'm going to deal with them, but first I have to deal with you.'

'You don't have to do this,' Alex said.

'Oh, but I do. This is the whole plan. I wanted to

bring you here so your husband would come looking for you. I have to get rid of you first, before I can deal with him and his friends.'

'You're outnumbered. What makes you think you can deal with them?'

'Lots of practice, dear. But I'm not that stupid that I think I can take on several men all by myself. That's why I have you. You're going to help me.'

Then she could smell it. The powerful smell of petrol.

'Don't worry, I've only poured a little bit. Just to get the fire going. I want them to come and try to get you before they all die.'

'Why are you trying to kill us?'

'Because you're sticking your nose in. I'm almost done now anyway. I work in threes. You two are part of my trifecta.'

'Who was the other one?'

'The pathologist, Valerie Hamilton. It's been fun, but I need to go.'

He left the room and they heard him thumping down the stairs.

Vern started pulling at the handcuffs holding her to the brass frame. 'Alex, do you think you can reach over? I have a pouch with handcuffs in it. There's a key in there too.'

Alex tried to stretch across, but she couldn't reach. 'Shit. I can't reach it.'

It was impossible and they both knew it.

'Oh fuck,' Vern said and knew what she had to try. She banged her hand against the wall. She winced in agony, then banged it even harder, once, twice and again and again, until finally she'd dislocated her thumb.

She screamed, thinking that she was going to pass out, but she kept it together.

Then she slipped her hand out of the handcuff.

FORTY-ONE

They got back in the Land Rover and Evans drove it the short distance up the hill, further into the woods. At the crest of the hill, they could see over to the loch, over the houses they had just been at.

'Something's bothering me,' Dunbar said. 'Gary Whitman's theory about the women having a mark on their hands. You know, the letter C and the marks to make it look like an X. I looked at some photos on the tech's camera.'

'And there was nothing there,' Evans said.

'Was I finished? Bloody jumping in. I bet you shout out the punchline to a joke as well.' Dunbar shook his head. 'Anyway, I was going to say, he was right. There was a mark near Carol's thumb.'

Harry was still in panic mode and he jumped out

of the car, so Muckle got out with Sparky and Evans leaped out. Dunbar followed.

They had stopped in front of a house with smoke coming out of its chimney. There were two other houses further along. Harry could see the top half of them and realised that they had been built on the other side of a rise.

Dunbar turned to him. 'Harry, we're going in here. I need you to stay outside. Just in case.'

Harry nodded, knowing what Dunbar was getting at: *in case Alex is dead.*

He walked away to the other houses, not wanting to see Jimmy's face when he came out with the news. He walked through the snow, heading up the rise, and crested it, not looking back. *Never look back,* his old man had said. The snow was coming down and he imagined how it would have felt if he had been here on holiday with Alex, sitting by a roaring fire, just him and her.

Then a thought hit him, something that Jimmy had just said.

Dunbar had looked at the photos of Carol's hands and seen the mark of a letter C on one. How had Gary Whitman known about this? Carol was already hanging by her neck when he got to her.

Harry reached the front door of the first house and the killer known as Infinity stepped out to greet him.

Albert Renfrew, the pathologist.

Or, as Harry knew him, Gary Whitman.

'Hello, Harry.' Gone was the East London accent.

'Time to give it up, Albert. We know all about you,' Harry said.

'I thought my impersonation of Gary Whitman was pretty good. But if you watch enough *EastEnders*, anybody can put on a fake accent.'

'I'm assuming Whitman existed, since we had you checked out and you passed. The documents were real.'

'I killed him and took his driving licence and his retired warrant card. He was getting too close. He and I talked one night over a few beers. All the things I said to you were the things he said to me. I couldn't believe how close he was.' Renfrew laughed.

'Did you have to kill Valerie Harper and Anderson Birrell?'

'Let's not forget about Dr Carter. I killed them all.'

'Why now?'

'Believe it or not, Valerie Henderson killed Caitlin McGhee thirty years ago. In a drunken fight. Carter and Birrell were also camp counsellors. We all covered for her. Then those two had a party in one of the houses one night, had some girls there. They were getting blootered. I spiked their drinks, the four of them. I killed the women. When Carter and Birrell woke up, they saw the girls were dead. I helped them bury them. The story was, they were having a drink and then they left together.'

'And nobody was any the wiser.'

'Correct. I figured that they were my insurance policy if they ever found out about me being a killer.'

'Why stop six years ago when Martin went to the psychiatric hospital?' Harry said.

'I didn't stop. I just killed in different ways. But then six months ago, I retired. I thought it would be fun to kill the girl I attacked six years ago and play with Martin's head.'

'You just chose him at random?'

Renfrew laughed. 'Of course not. I dated his mother thirty years ago. I wanted to marry her, but her father stopped me. Then she got pregnant by some arsehole, who skipped off when he found out. I just wanted the old man to think his grandson was a psycho killer. Worked, didn't it? But now I'm retired and away from the pathology game, killing would be harder, since I won't be working with the police. Time to move on. I just wanted to wrap things up. One last round of killing around Christmastime. Finally have them put Martin away for good. Then I would be off.'

'You had it all figured out. Why kill the others? Valerie and Dr Carter and Birrell?'

'Valerie moved away, then came back to take up my

position. I was worried she would start talking with those other two idiots. If she'd only stayed away. Then you lot were supposed to think Gary Whitman was responsible. That he'd wormed his way in with you and had made a fool of you. Then he would have disappeared. I killed him so I could take his persona, put the police on his trail. They would never find him, of course, because I buried him. I'd be off, a free man.'

'We got in your way, though. You let us catch you when you were pretending to be Whitman so you could manipulate us.'

'Worked, didn't it?'

'For a little while,' Harry said. 'But where's Alex? And Vern?'

'Close. They're not dead. I just used them to draw you here. And now you've caught me fair and square. But just one thing before you take me in.'

Renfrew brought his hand out from his inside pocket and Harry watched helplessly as he lit a rag that had been soaked in something flammable and threw it into the house, where it caught the petrol he'd poured.

'Here I am, Harry. Arrest me. Then read about how they found the charred corpse of your wife and her friend upstairs.'

'You're bluffing.'

They both heard the screams from the upper floor.

'Your choice, Harry. Fight with me and try to arrest me, or go try and save your wife. What's it to be?'

'You bastard.'

Renfrew looked him in the eyes. 'Don't worry; we'll meet again, Harry.' He turned and ran round the back.

Harry ran into the house.

FORTY-TWO

They searched the house, room by room, with Sparky itching to have a go. There was evidence of somebody having been here. Recent packages in the kitchen. The smell of cooking. But it was the fire dying out in the grate that was the big clue.

'Get upstairs, Muckle,' said Dunbar. 'Let the dug have the bastard if he's there.'

'Come on, boy.' Muckle led the way up, knowing full well he'd step in front of the dog if the killer had a knife in his hand. Muckle had been in many a knife fight and would have a go himself before he'd risk his dog.

As it turned out, the only knife that was upstairs was a butter knife on the floor in one of the bedrooms.

'Nobody here!' he shouted after checking the other rooms.

Dunbar and Evans came up and had a look around.

'Somebody's been here,' said Muckle. 'The logs in the fire are still burning. They can't be that far away.'

They went back downstairs and Dunbar's phone rang.

'Jimmy? It's David.'

'Hello, son. What's up?'

'I was going back over some things I'd researched and I was looking at Gary Whitman. I'd only peeked inside the Met's database. And the DVLA's. But I was doing more research for the book and I came across a little story you might find interesting.'

'What's that?'

'Gary Whitman went missing six months ago. He's never been found.'

'But we know he's here. Did he just drop off the radar or something?'

'I don't think so. When you told me about Albert Renfrew, I googled him and looked at images. He looks almost identical to Whitman. Dark hair, dark beard, almost the same build. If they were standing side by side, you'd notice a difference. But not if you looked at a crappy ID photo. I think Renfrew was masquerading as Whitman with you lot because you didn't know Renfrew. Then if people who knew Renfrew saw him, well, it's just Renfrew, isn't it? They wouldn't ask ques-

tions. As long as you didn't see him at the same time as the others.'

'Thanks, David. We'll talk later.' Dunbar hung up and looked at Muckle and Evans.

'That bloke we were interviewing? Gary Whitman? He's not Gary Whitman. He's Albert Renfrew, the pathologist. That bastard's been playing us.'

They ran downstairs and out of the house. Dunbar looked along the track.

One of the other houses was on fire.

FORTY-THREE

The fire spread in the open-plan living area, the petrol lighting up quickly. The flames spread towards the stairs over to one side of the big room, taking hold of the wood.

Harry knew this house was going to be engulfed in minutes. Maybe that was the real reason they'd shut the place down; it was a death trap.

He tried to run into in to the living room but Renfrew had poured the petrol strategically so the stairs would burn first, preventing escape.

'Alex! Vern! Are you up there?'

He heard a scream again. Somebody was up there.

'Help us! We're up here! We're trapped.'

Harry took his jacket off and started slapping at the flames, but it was no good. The fire was intense and growing more intense with every passing second. He looked at the stairs and knew he couldn't get up that way.

He ran outside to see if there was a way to get up to the next level. A drainpipe to climb. Anything.

He saw Vern at a window, and then suddenly the glass exploded outwards. He covered his head as the glass rained down on him.

Then Robbie Evans came firing in, driving the Land Rover like he was on drugs.

'They're up there!' Harry shouted, and Evans rammed the big car into the house sideways. He, Dunbar, Muckle and the dog jumped out and suddenly Evans was climbing on top of the big car.

Vern was knocking out the small shards of glass when Harry saw Alex appear at the window. Vern helped her get her leg over and get out. Evans got hold of her and then reached his hands up to grab Vern as she climbed out.

She screamed as he grabbed her hand. 'Thumb dislocated,' she said.

Alex slid down the windscreen onto the bonnet and was helped off by Harry. Vern and Evans leaped off the side into the snow. Dunbar had got behind the wheel and he floored it away from the house, while the others made it across the track to safety, where they watched the house burn down.

'Gary Whitman disappeared six months ago,' Dunbar explained to Harry.

'I know. Renfrew told me he killed Whitman.'

'You spoke to him?'

Harry nodded, out of breath. 'I could have arrested him, but he'd thrown the petrol-soaked rag in after he lit it. I had to try to get Alex.'

'I understand. Fuck 'im. Alex and Vern are safe, that's the main thing.'

Muckle came over and Sparky nuzzled Alex.

'The fire brigade are on their way,' he said. 'Although I doubt there will be much left to put out. Maybe some burning bushes.'

'Maybe the whole fucking forest, the way it's going,' Dunbar said. He turned to Robbie. 'Good job there. I haven't seen you move that fast in a long time.'

'I had a broken ankle, remember?'

'That excuse won't wash now. Time you were taking us lads to the bar and putting your hand in your pocket.'

'Aye, and the moon might be made of cheese.'

'We could always go to the chippie.' Dunbar turned to Muckle. 'You ever been to the chippie along from our station?'

'Aye. Many a time. The one where Linda Fry works?'

'That's the one.'

'I don't know why we're talking about the chippie,' Evans said. 'Anybody fancy a pint?'

FORTY-FOUR

The snow had stopped falling, as if it knew they were leaving.

'The invitation's open to all of you,' Dunbar said. 'Cathy's pal has rented a hall and it's going to be a belter of a Hogmanay. I'm just glad we're getting to go instead of being stuck up here.'

They were in Shug's living room.

'We'll be there,' David said.

'And remember what I said. January second, we can have a coffee and a chat about your book. January first will be over by the time I sober up.'

'Terrific. We'll be packing soon. Our lease is up on Hogmanay and then we're heading to Glasgow. Muckle's coming along.'

'You sure you don't want to come with us?' Muckle asked Vern.

Her thumb was in a brace. The doctor had managed to get it back into place and he didn't think she'd need surgery. 'I'm riding back down with Jimmy and Robbie.' She smiled at Evans.

'Just carry some extra braces with you, hen,' Dunbar said. 'I've got a crash helmet.'

'You wear a crash helmet every day 'cause you're daft,' Evans said.

'You've taken that too far. There are people who wear helmets.' Dunbar shook his head. 'You sure you want to come down in our Land Rover?' he asked Vern.

'I'm sure.'

'You'll get to see Robbie squealing like a wee lassie when he thinks I've fallen asleep at the wheel.'

'He does a great impression of somebody snoring at the wheel too,' said Evans.

'Shut your hole,' said Dunbar. 'I was congested, that's all.'

They talked about how Albert Renfrew, a.k.a. Gary Whitman, had escaped in the hearse, which had been found abandoned in a little industrial park's car park. Every force in the UK was looking for him.

'Well, we're going to head off,' Harry said.

'Take care, you two,' Dunbar said.

They said their goodbyes and got into Alex's Audi, Harry behind the wheel.

'I was lying awake in bed this morning wondering if I should find a new career,' she said.

'Why?'

'How many times is it that I've landed in trouble? Good God, it can only happen to me. I'm going to run out of luck one day.'

'Rubbish. You make a great detective.'

Harry pulled away and drove down to the main road and headed south.

He didn't mention Renfrew's last words to him.

We'll meet again, Harry.

There would be a time to worry.

Today wasn't it.

AFTERWORD

Well, here we are again at the end of another Harry McNeil novel. I hope you enjoyed this one as much as the others. If I could ask you to leave a review or a rating on Amazon, that would be fantastic. I appreciate every one of them, and it helps to keep me writing.

Thank you to my wife and daughters, for keeping me sane. To Bear and Bella, who keep me sane in their own way. To my group of readers with huge thanks. It's nice to know I'm not on this journey alone. Also to Ruth from Police Scotland.

And thanks to you, the reader, for reading my books. I couldn't do this without you.

All the best my friends.

    John Carson

    December 2020

    New York

Printed in Great Britain
by Amazon

37234819R00142